Black Beans & Venom

A Carol Sabala Mystery

Vinnie Hansen

Black Beans & Venom
A Carol Sabala Mystery

Published by: Misterio Press
www.misteriopress.com

Although a private family in Cuban distributes blue scorpion venom as a cancer cure, the family in this story is fictional, as are all the characters. If any characters bear any resemblance to actual persons, living or dead, the resemblance is coincidental. All the incidents in this work are products of the author's imagination.

Cover art by Book Cover Corner, www.bookcovercorner.com

Background cover artwork: Daniel S. Friedman

ISBN-10: 0991320891

ISBN-13: 978-0-9913208-9-9

Hansen, Vinnie.

Black Beans & Venom / Vinnie Hansen — 1st ed.

To Daniel Stuart Friedman, my husband

PRAISE FOR HANSEN'S WORK

Black Beans & Venom – Claymore Award Finalist.

"Her writing style is like liquid poetry. Her characters rule the page, and the action moves smoothly from one scene to the next."
Midwest Book Review

"I love Carol Sabala...quirky, gutsy and my kind of gal in an aqua tank top."
--Cara Black, Author of the Aimée Leduc mystery series

"Hansen's sense of humor and protagonist make for a good read. I particularly enjoyed her faithfully rendered Santa Cruz background."
--Laura Crum, author of the Gail McCarthy murder mystery series

"The pacing of Hansen's story is excellent."
--Chris Watson, *Santa Cruz Sentinel* on *Murder, Honey*

"I just finished Murder, Honey *and I found it splendid."*
--Laura Davis, author of *Courage to Heal*

"With edgy precision, Hansen applies all the elements of a good mystery: interesting plot, compelling characters, a finely drawn sense of place, and excellent writing. One Tough Cookie *has made me a fan, one who can't wait to gorge on* Rotten Dates.*"*
--Denise Osborne, author of *Feng Shui Mysteries* and Queenie Davilov Mysteries

"In Sabala, Hansen has created a likable sleuth whose many problems readers may readily identify with, and as far as Carol's mother goes—well, let's just say I hope we see more of her in the future."
--Michael Cornelius, *The Bloomsbury Review*

"Five silver pens out of five for 'Tang Is Not Juice.'*"*
--Silas Spaeth, *Salinas Californian*

"Best Book of Fiction of 2005" for Tang Is Not Juice
Oklahoma Writers' Federation, Inc.

ALSO BY VINNIE HANSEN:

Murder, Honey

One Tough Cookie

Rotten Dates

Tang Is Not Juice

Death with Dessert

Art, Wine & Bullets

Anything is possible in Havana.

Graham Greene

THE SCORPION AND THE FROG

A scorpion decided to visit his cousin and set off on his journey. He came upon a river. Unable to swim, he was contemplating turning back when he spotted a frog on the river bank.

"Mr. Frog," he asked, "would you please let me ride on your back across the river?"

"But, Mr. Scorpion, how do I know you won't sting me and kill me?"

"Of course I won't sting you. If I kill you, you will drown and so will I because I can't swim," the scorpion argued.

This made sense, but the frog was still suspicious. "How do I know you won't kill me when we get to the other side?"

"Ahh...," the scorpion said smoothly, "I would be so grateful for your help, how could I possibly sting you?"

The frog, a gentle creature, admitted that he could not imagine anyone acting in such a manner, so he agreed to carry the scorpion across the river. Half way across the rushing water, the frog felt the sharp sting on his back. As he started to go numb, the frog shouted, "Why did you do that? Now we'll both die!"

"I couldn't help it," the scorpion said. "It's my nature."

(Sometimes attributed to Aesop,
the origin of this fable is not actually known.)

November, 2001

CHAPTER ONE

I liked J.J. Sloan better as a practicing alcoholic. At least then, I knew where to find him, right down to which stool he would occupy. Now that he had renewed his commitments to running and recovery, he was not only less reachable, but also more insufferable, which I had not thought possible.

"That's the glory of cross-country running," he crowed, as he stood in the office, dipping one knee and then the other to stretch his Achilles tendons. "Your legs can take you anywhere." He pronounced this as though he were Neil Armstrong, taking the first step on the moon on behalf of all mankind. Next he stretched his hamstrings by bending at the waist and reaching for his shins. He had good legs, I would give him that, but they could not compensate for the crooked nose and acne-scarred skin.

"File that pile, Carol." Without further ado, he trotted to the door and down the hallway.

I fumed in our windowless office. Even though J.J. had taken me on as a favor to my boyfriend David and had invested hundreds of hours training me to be a private investigator, it felt insulting to have him continue to treat me like a peon. Yet Sloan's Investigative Services was his business, if you could call it that.

The office existed as a place to receive messages and to burn coffee. Our bread and butter jobs were doing legwork for attorneys. We went to them. Other clients usually called before coming to the office. The light on the phone wasn't blinking, though. J.J. must have already listened to our messages; either that or we were even more unpopular than usual.

The place stank from the coffee tar at the bottom of the pot. I filled it with hot water and left it in the bathroom sink for J.J. to deal with, since he was the one who had cooked the coffee down to paste.

I picked up a stapled sheaf from the untidy mound on J.J.'s desk. At least when J.J. was at the bar, I could waltz right in and talk to him. I couldn't do that when he was at an AA meeting, and I wasn't about to chase him up and down the hills by the university. Plus, when he was drunk, J.J. thought logically. Now every idea filtered through the Twelve Steps. Furthermore, when he was a practicing alcoholic, he remembered to pay me.

I took a deep breath, counting to eight on the inhalation, trying to calm my temper. My mom had always said it would get me into trouble, and for the most part she had been right. The red fire in my nature served me, though, when I was under attack, which happened in my line of work.

But I would be damned if I'd file J.J.'s papers for free. As I swung the deposition in my hand toward the pile, several loose sheets fanned into the air. I considered leaving them on the floor.

My inflated sense of fairness kicked in. I was being petty. I had caused the mess. I got down on my hands and knees to fish out a paper that had glided under J.J.'s desk. As I stretched my arm, butt aimed at the door like someone in a contorted yoga position, the most amazing thing happened. Someone entered our office.

I knew it wasn't J.J. since there was no immediate crack about my ass. Also, from my perspective, I could see a pair of alligator pumps and the ankles and calves of shapely legs shimmery in nylon stockings. So, unless J.J. had taken up a new enterprise, I deduced that we had a customer.

I backed out, stood, and brushed off the knees of my jeans while taking in the apparition. The woman held an alligator purse and modeled a peachy cashmere twinset accented with a double strand of pearls and matching earrings below sweeping, coifed gold hair. She was très chic for the era of Jackie O, and yet I doubted she was aiming for a retro look.

She sniffed.

"Burnt coffee," I explained.

"Possibly," she said enigmatically, as though she'd picked up another scent—the toilet, perhaps.

I returned the paper I was clutching, a past due notice from Pacific Gas and Electric, to J.J.'s desk, placing it upside down.

"Can I help you?"

"I'm Lucille Barnhart." She waited as though the name were supposed to mean something. "This is a private investigating firm?"

Firm. I liked that. "Sloan Investigative Services."

"Are you Sloan?" She had not moved, keeping the door within arm's reach.

"Private investigator Carol Sabala, at your service."

I stepped toward her and extended my hand. She looked at it and then at the floor.

"Oh, yeah. Sorry." I wiped off my hands on my pants, but a snob force shield stopped me from proffering to shake again.

Her disgust was enough to cause fine wrinkles in her fully made-up mask. "Is that a Mexican name?"

I bristled like a pot scrubber. God. In addition to being a time-warp freak, the potential client was an impertinent bigot.

Everyone was a bit bigoted, but the impertinent part got my goat. "*Sí, señora.*" *Oh, great, Carol. You couldn't help yourself, could you?*

The woman didn't blink. Did not move at all. "So, you speak Spanish, too?"

I rocked my hand in the air. "Passably." Where was this going? I studied her. With the sixties garb and collagen lips, she could be anywhere from my age—mid forties—to seventy.

"That could be handy."

"Would you like a seat?" I gestured toward the straight-backed chair in front of my desk.

She glanced at it.

So did I. "Let me get a napkin to wipe it off."

I walked behind J.J.'s desk to our microwave and coffee machine counter. Beside the microwave was the plastic wrap of a jumbo bag of napkins. Empty. Of course. I went into the bathroom. I didn't think our potential client would approve of me wiping her chair with toilet paper, so I fetched the hand towel. It was only moderately dirty. I folded it inside out and went to wipe the film of dust from the wooden chair.

Once I had created a safe haven and pulled out the chair like a gentleman at a restaurant, the woman sat, upright, on its edge. I took a seat. She propped bejeweled hands atop her bag, perfect coppery nails facing in my direction. "Do you handle missing persons?"

"Of course." I thought of the way I'd tracked down my own long-absent father. "That's my specialty." *You have to sell yourself,* David would say. I slid a yellow legal pad in front of me and extracted a pen from the mug on my desk. "Who's missing?"

"My daughter."

"Her name?"

"Megan Elizabeth Melquist."

"How long has she been missing?"

"Two months."

"Two months? Aren't the police involved?"

The mother sighed long and deep. "My daughter is thirty-two years old and there's no sign of 'foul play.' In their words, they can't investigate every young woman who decides to go off on a trip and doesn't call her mom."

"A trip? So you know where Megan went?"

"Cuba."

"Cuba." I jotted it down even though all the promise of the case had slipped away before I wrote the C. No wonder the woman had liked the fact I spoke Spanish, but how in the world would I find someone in *Cuba*? It was becoming clearer and clearer why the police department had not gotten involved. "Did you expect Megan to contact you?"

This woman did not wiggle or squirm, but rather grew stiller. "I would *expect* her to contact me, yes."

"Does that mean you expected Megan to do things but she didn't?" I was beginning to sense why Megan might have taken off.

The woman gave me a hard stare, her light brown eyes coppery as her nails. "Megan likes to think she's an independent young woman. An adventurer. She's not an ordinary girl."

Of course not. She also isn't a girl. "So why don't you believe she is just off having an adventure?"

"No doubt she is."

"Then she's not a missing person?"

"Just tell me, Carol Sabala, private investigator, can you locate my daughter?"

Thoughts swirled through my head. The woman's obvious money and our unpaid Pacific Gas and Electric bill. David's nagging on me to sell myself. The desire for an exciting case rather than the grunt-work filing and stakeouts J.J. dished out to me.

"Sure," I said.

The woman unclasped her handbag and withdrew a checkbook. In matching alligator, of course.

September, 2001 – Two Months Earlier

CHAPTER TWO

Megan peered through the peephole. Eric rocked side to side on the concrete walkway in front of her apartment door. A goofy grin split his tanned face.

"Babe, let me in," he pleaded. "Look at what I brought you." A fistful of long-stemmed red roses shot up into view. "Your favorite."

She swung the door open, but not because of the flowers. She had not told him it was over, instead she'd avoided him and left his calls unanswered. She needed to tell him straight up. A person didn't shout a break-up through a doorway, creating a drama that could be misconstrued. She wanted to stare calmly into his eyes, let him see that she was not afraid, that she was clear and rational and meant it. Let him take in her unmade-up face, pale and pasty from chemo, and her worn flannel PJs bagging around her frame. That should help convince him that she no longer cared.

As he glided into the room, she positioned herself behind the counter. It separated the galley kitchen from the living area.

"Babe, I'm sorry if I pissed you off." He extended the roses over the faux wood surface, and she accepted them. He tried to touch her hand, but she jerked it away. His cat-like eyes glinted.

She extracted scissors from a drawer and snipped the stems, leaving the scissors on the counter.

"Aren't you going to put those in a vase?"

"Later." She dumped the flowers in the sink, stirring their intoxicating perfume. In spite of the man across from her, she drew in the fragrance. Shakespeare was right. The roses, players in a pure shit scene, smelled as sweet.

He drummed his fingers along the arch of the faucet. "Aren't you going to say thank you?"

"No." She bit her lower lip, chapped from chemo, or maybe from worried chewing. She watched him, images of her life before Eric flitting through her skull, all the guys at the bar—the alcoholics, and married dudes, and ordinary, boring guys in sports jerseys.

"Look, babe, I'm sorry if I hurt you."

Involuntarily she fingered the red nick on her pale neck. In spite of her resolve, her fingers quivered against her flesh. Her fingertips traced the small distance to her carotid artery, throbbing with life.

"It was a fantasy," Eric said. "Just sexual role playing."

Ah, he was clever, one of the first things she'd loved about him. He dove into her like a pearl diver and struck straight down to that girl at the bottom of her sea—a reclusive mermaid who had remained a virgin into college, who wondered always how far from normal she was, who longed to be something else, a siren, perhaps, fearless, dangerous even.

"It went too far." Her voice was hoarse.

"Yes, but you took it too literally."

"I had a knife to my neck! How do you not take that literally?"

He jacked himself onto the counter and swung to her side—quick and smooth as an action hero.

She backed against the oven on the far side of the narrow space.

Putting a finger to her lips, he crooned, "Shhhhhhh," tender as a father with a baby. He traced her mouth.

Behind him on the counter, the scissors sparked with reflected light. She crabbed away toward the refrigerator.

Confusion roiled in her. He remained a yard away, so handsome. Back when her hair fell out in clumps and her face bloated from cortisone, he had stayed, undisturbed by her disintegration, comfortable with it. He gazed at her now as though she were as lovely as Venus.

She met his eyes. His Hawaiian shirt draped on relaxed shoulders. He stretched out a hand again. "It's me, babe." One fingertip tracked along her forearm.

"Don't." She backed away, the doubts percolating. She'd been walking down this road with Eric, excited to explore her sexuality. She was partly to blame for where it had lead. Eric had coaxed her forward, but memories had prodded her from behind: her teenaged friend Brittany teasing her that she hadn't even been fingered, then six years married to Mr. Missionary Position. Eric had thrilled her, aroused her even now.

She realized too late that she'd stepped out of reach of the scissors.

He lunged. His weight plunged into her center of gravity. Her hip slammed onto the linoleum. Her fists cranked like a hay baler until he pinned her arms. As she struggled and he slapped her face, she wondered if it was her fault. He didn't know she'd called it quits.

She bucked underneath him. "Stop!"

He released one of her pinned arms long enough to slap her again, so hard her brain shook inside her head. The elasticized waistband of her pajamas slid over her hips with one forceful yank.

When Eric finished, he panted in her ear, "I love you."

She'd waited for months to hear those magic words. Now that he had said them, her body froze with fear.

The weight released from on top of her. Standing, he wiped himself with one of her cloth napkins and tossed the wad onto the floor. He pulled up his pants and smoothed down his shirt. "Don't even think of leaving me."

He hefted the scissors from the counter, snorted, and snick-snacked them in front of her face. Jerking open the drawer, he threw them inside and slammed it shut. He tossed one of the roses onto her pounding heart. Then he strolled to the door and left.

She stood up shaking. She'd let the situation spin out of control. Stumbling to the bathroom, she grasped the edges of the sink and inspected herself. His hand had imprinted a red pattern on her pale cheek. She rinsed off her face. Her bottom stung. She sat on the toilet and used a hand mirror to check herself. Her labia swelled in purple blooms, but she saw no rips or blood.

Sure she could get a restraining order—exactly the move to incite him, to make her end up dead. She wasn't fighting cancer so she could die from bad taste in men.

In the magazine basket next to her, rested the travel book about Cuba, stuffed with computer print outs about alternative medicine there. The universe had announced—screamed at her actually—that it was time to go.

October, 2001

CHAPTER THREE

Eric Mars had delivered a mint-condition Willie Mays card. He was flush with cash and it was time to celebrate. He crossed the schoolyard. Silhouetted in the darkening sky, two distant palm trees poked over the classroom like goalposts. The schoolteacher often worked here into dusk.

The classroom door opened onto the quad. He could tell by the size of the desks that she taught little kids, maybe first grade. She looked the part, young and innocent, with golden hair and rosy cheeks—a little chubby, like one of those images on a Valentine's card—what were they called—like a cherub? His body tingled at the idea of her, a sweet treat he'd been saving.

He filled the lighted doorway with his body and smiled. The teacher whirled from a white board where she'd been crouched, drawing flowers with markers. He didn't even know markers came in those colors—pink and purple and lime green.

"Can I help you?" Her voice sounded dry.

He watched the eyes flicking up and down and even as her body tensed, he knew she registered his handsomeness, the thick wavy hair and ripped body, because women always noticed. He had broad shoulders by nature, but it took work to have a washboard stomach. The teacher blushed. They never wanted to admit how attracted they were to danger, to wild, feral creatures. He thought about shoving her onto all fours and mounting her like an animal.

He took her in, mostly trusting, but growing frightened, her eyes darting around the room now, to the windows, the phone, the broom propped in a corner. But his cock did not swell with excitement. He turned and left her there, cowering, and he hadn't done a thing. Not one prosecutable thing. Yet he had abandoned her there, terrified and wondering.

The anticipated shiver of pleasure failed to arrive. He stalked across the green field, clenching his fists in frustration. It was Megan's fault. She was poison. She'd ruined him.

The antidote suggested itself, first as a whisper, then as a certainty. The anger passed, and his sweet, Zen calm replaced it. He smiled into the descending darkness.

November, 2001

CHAPTER FOUR

"Are you out of your mind?" J.J. asked. Sobriety had clipped his tolerance for risk. "You accepted a retainer for that!"

To stay on his good side, I had filed the whole stack on his desk, except for the overdue payment notices, which I had placed front and center. But this ploy had been for naught. He stood scowling behind his desk in his red running shorts and gray sweat-soaked Redwings tee shirt holding the folded, dust-covered bathroom towel. He had also encountered the coffee pot full of black water in the sink.

I snapped the check in front of his eyes, but he merely tossed the towel toward the bathroom floor and used the bottom of his tee shirt to mop his face. "It's illegal to go to Cuba. Did you know that when you accepted this woman's money?"

In the old days, legality never would have been J.J.'s lead argument. "Not technically illegal," I said. "Restricted."

"No American airline even flies there."

I held the check closer to his eyes, so he could read the amount. The woman, Lucille Barnhart, had not even asked our usual rates. She had calmly written a Vanguard check for ten thousand dollars and slid it across the desk. "That's a retainer. Let me know when you need more."

J.J. absorbed the zeros. "How would you get there?"

The answer to that turned out to be not easily. As I spent the afternoon at my office computer and phone, what had seemed like an impressively large retainer quickly dwindled. I could purchase a ticket to and from Cancun easily enough, but I had to work with a travel agency out of the country for the ticket from Cancun to Havana. That was an hour trip, but cost as much as the twenty-five-hundred-mile trip from the San Francisco International Airport to Cancun, Mexico. However, with Lucille Barnhart as a client, I did not expect money to be a problem. There were greater obstacles. The first was David's resistance.

"J.J. only wants you to go for the money."

"Well derrr." I chopped onions for the spaghetti sauce, rocking the long blade and showing off the skills I'd acquired at my other job at the swanky restaurant Archibald's. My eyes teared. "It's unfair to push me to be more assertive, but then not to support me when I reel in a challenging case."

"Not challenging, Carol—illegal."

"Not technically."

David washed mushrooms by shaking them in a plastic bag full of salty water, another cooking tip I'd learned at Archibald's. "It's dangerous. Especially now."

"Castro and communists had nothing to do with the World Trade Center."

I knew that I was stating the obvious, and that this was not David's point. His point was that two months after 9/11 did not seem like the best time to travel to a place unfriendly to the United States. We were living in a time when even people in

Santa Cruz, a bastion of liberalism, were driving around with American flags flapping from their vehicles. People were on edge. Security at airports had been heightened.

My frustration sizzled like the onions in the skillet. It stemmed partly from David's hypocrisy of pushing me in my career, only to pull back at a challenging case, and partly from the truth of his statement. From my afternoon at the computer, I'd learned a person could be fined or thrown in jail for traveling to Cuba, unless you went through the proper channels and obtained permission for a limited cultural or humanitarian trip. I did not see myself doing that.

"Technically it's not illegal to go to Cuba." I stirred the onions as he painstakingly cut the mushrooms. I winced at the way he wielded the knife. "Curl your fingers under." It required maximum restraint not to hijack his job. "It's just illegal to spend money there."

To this assertion he rolled his eyes. "Why does this woman want you to find her daughter? How does she know what's her name went to Cuba?"

"Megan Elizabeth." I didn't have an answer for his real question, the woman's motive. I'd accepted Lucille Barnhart's retainer, but I had legwork to do before I cashed the check.

Still, after the stunt David had pulled on my last big case, an action that had nearly destroyed our relationship, he would not press his point. After a year of reflection, we both knew the trouble between us was bigger than David's one decision last year. We'd both been so self-absorbed, David with showing his photography at a big art tour and me with The Big Case, that we had missed each other's cues. We had been so preoccupied that we didn't find time to take bike rides together, to rest in the meadows and talk. We barely found time for sex. I knew, too, that David had honestly felt his actions were a win/win situation; he had acted from obtuseness, not malice. Yet after a year, neither of us was completely comfortable.

The wealth of Lucille Barnhart's house matched her clothing. She lived in a two-story Mediterranean-style villa on Opal Cliff Drive. The ocean side. My shoes sank into pale carpet as I gravitated to a wall of windows with an unobstructed view of the Pacific from Capitola to Pleasure Point. I looked down on the backs of wetsuited surfers, beds of rocking kelp, sailboats in the distance. Even with the windows closed, the lullaby of the surf filled the silence of the house. Lucille remained across the room, the view an everyday occurrence for her.

What would it be like to live in this grandeur? My first impression was that it would be like living in a beautiful empty conch shell with all its hardness and delicate, fragile edges, full of ocean sound.

Lucille Barnhart ushered me to a cozy den off the living room where she, or perhaps a maid, had set out a flower-painted porcelain teapot with matching dainty teacups on saucers. The sugar and milk in matching bowl and pitcher, lemon wedges on a matching plate, real silverware, rose-colored linen napkins, and a dish of tiny shortbread cookies filled me with a weird emotional tug of war. The setting was opulent and excessive, but for all that, I could not deny its appeal. The woman tucked her gray wool skirt under her and perched primly as she offered to pour me a cup of tea. Beside her lay a manila envelope.

"My own blend." Today she wore a cream-colored silk shell and filigreed gold earrings and necklace, her hair pulled into a chignon. There was something lovely, elegant and completely odd about the woman.

Many houses lined the mile or so of Opal Cliff Drive. If I walked down Lucille's slate driveway, some of the neighbors would be out taking advantage of this warm November day, but none of them would be dressed like her. They would be wearing baggy pants or long beach shorts, sweatshirts from O'Neill's, flip flops or athletic shoes, rendering them indistinguishable from the surfers living in converted garages on nearby Pleasure

Point. Lucille donned hose on a Saturday afternoon.

I sipped the piping hot tea. "Mmmm. Blackberry?"

"I did put in a berry," she said, "but there are also two types of mint and a pinch of chamomile."

"Delicious." I didn't know how to broach my topic. I carefully set the cup back onto its saucer before I stained the loveseat.

"I'm astounded at the ticket price from Cancun to Cuba, but don't worry." Lucille gestured vaguely at the room and house beyond. "Money is not an issue, thanks to my dearly departed." She stirred milk into her tea and then left it sitting.

I should have booked first class. "You have a different name than Megan. Is she married?"

"Divorced."

"Is her husband on the scene?"

"Remarried with kids and living in New Jersey."

"Does Megan have children?"

"No." For a moment only the surf sounded in the room. She lifted her teacup, and the delicate rattle seemed loud. The cup remained posed in the air. "There's no need to ask me these questions, Ms. Sabala. After you agreed to take the case, I returned home and gathered all the information you will need." She placed the cup back in its saucer and patted the manila envelope.

I clamped teeth on my lower lip, dug fingernails into my palm, and began a mental loop of J.J.'s admonition, "Do not bite the hand that feeds you." The woman was trying to be helpful, but I hated her assumption that she knew what my investigation would require. One final question on the subject spilled out. "Why did she keep the name Melquist?"

The mother regarded me coldly. "She said she liked it better."

Megan Elizabeth Melquist did sound more melodic than Megan Elizabeth Barnhart, but still—ouch.

I hurriedly switched to a more business-like question. "How do you know Megan is in Cuba?"

Her gaze dropped, but popped back up to meet mine. "Another agency uncovered that information. Megan purchased a ticket from here to Vancouver to Nassau and from there to Havana."

"Another detective agency?" Internally I chanted J.J.'s platitude, "The customer is always right." When it came to running his business, J.J. was as full of aphorisms as my mother had been.

"An agency in San Francisco." She sipped her tea with her pinky extended.

I had pushed for a meeting in her home rather than in our office to get a better feel for my client and what I might be taking on. It had not been much of a battle. Lucille probably had no desire to return to our dingy office. "Were you unhappy with their work?" I asked.

"Not at all. They were very professional."

"And, so...?" I arched my eyebrows, raised my delicate teacup, and inhaled the aroma, careful not to spill on the cream and mauve stripes of the loveseat.

"No one in that agency was willing to travel to Cuba."

"Perhaps because for our purposes, it would be illegal."

"One can obtain a visa for a humanitarian visit."

"So you're proposing I deliver a case of Aspirin?"

Lucille's eyes became steely, reminiscent of my grandmother's. My grandmother had been the disapproving type, and I was the type to incite disapproval. Lucille's frank regard shriveled my insides and made me feel like a dried up cow patty. She may have given me a retainer, but she was not about to subject herself to the questions of a self-invited "guest" in sneakers. "Aren't these obstacles the reason one hires a private investigator?"

"Obstacles?" I sipped, slurping a little, maybe on purpose. "You mean illegal activities?"

"Not illegal." She winced. "Let's say to operate in the gray areas."

"Fine. Gray areas." *As in shady.* "It has been months since Megan disappeared. Why do you think she's still in Cuba? Has there been a paper trail?"

"American credit cards are useless in Cuba. Before she left, Megan cashed out a five-thousand-dollar CD even though it wasn't mature." Her lips tightened in a moue of disgust. I guess at the idea of paying an early withdrawal penalty. "Please look over the contents of this envelope. That should eliminate your need to interrogate me."

My gaze traveled to the envelope in her hands, but I didn't reach for it. "Mrs. Barnhart, why, exactly, do you want me to track Megan down?"

"She's my daughter." Her diction was as crisp as snapping scissors. But then she looked away, out toward the grand view, the gentle rocking waves.

The sound of the ocean filled the room and tugged at my blood. No matter what else I thought of this woman, she was a mother, and no matter how chilly or smothering she might have been, she apparently loved her daughter. I knew something about these types of relationships—not that my mother had been smothering—quite the opposite, but she had been a strong force against which I'd battled to define myself.

"But Megan is a grown woman—an adult." I destroyed the sentimental reverie. "What am I supposed to do if I find her?"

"Let me know she is alive."

"We're all dying," Brittany Bañuelos hissed at me across the bank counter.

That was her response to my question, "Is Megan Melquist dying?"

The lapel pin on Brittany's navy blue blazer identified her as Assistant Branch Manager, which meant glorified clerk. She had the same long, wavy, unruly hair I once had except hers was dark and tied back with a wide white ribbon, not a style I had ever adopted. For a second I mourned my missing hair, even though I now loved my wash-and-wear very short curls.

"I can't believe Lucille sent you here to question me."

It was shocking, but Lucille had not known where Brittany

Bañuelos, Megan's supposed best friend, lived, and the former San Francisco investigator had not provided her home address, either. However, her place of employment had been in their reports. Now Brittany Bañuelos glared at me, and then pointedly eyed the line snaking toward the door.

"I'm at work," she said, in case I had not noticed.

"Just a couple of questions and then I'll vamoose."

She closed her teller station and motioned me to the side of their corral. Off her stool, she was short, about five foot two, and round. "You picked the worst time—opening hour on a Monday."

"Okay, then, to get to the point, why would someone with breast cancer travel to Cuba?"

"To find a miracle."

"If you want me to leave, I need answers I can understand."

"If I want you to leave, I will call security."

I was beginning to like Brittany Bañuelos.

"You met Lucille," she said after a moment. This wasn't a clear response to my question, but I certainly understood the innuendo dripping from the simple sentence.

"She hired me."

"Then you'll understand when I tell you that Megan went to Cuba to escape. And who knows, she might find the cure she's seeking."

"She went to Cuba to find a cure for cancer?" This seemed to be what Brittany was saying, but it was too absurd to register. I felt like I had drunk cough syrup for breakfast.

"Blue scorpion venom." Brittany shook her head.

"Blue scorpion venom?" I madly scribbled the unbelievable words.

"The way I understand it, these scorpions exist only in Cuba." Brittany glanced at the lengthening line of people, bent into a full S. "Look. Megan's cancer did not respond to chemo. It had been metastasizing." Brittany's eyes misted. She leaned toward me and whispered ferociously, "And Lucille is such a bitch." Brittany pulled away from my ear, but continued to whisper. "She thinks of Megan as some helpless creature. No matter what Megan wanted, she pushed and pushed for more aggressive treatment like money could buy Megan's life." Brittany turned. "I have to go back to work." She snatched a bank brochure from a plastic display and used a chained pen to jot down a phone number. "My cell. Call me. Before you try to find Megan, I have to tell you about Eric Mars." She handed me the paper. "Please do not come back here."

I watched Brittany snatch a tissue and dab her eyes on her way back to her station. She seemed like a good friend to have—bland maybe, but sensible and down to earth. The type missing from my repertoire.

But I understood Lucille, too. What mother would not be hell bent on saving her child's life? Her only child. From the packet of information Lucille had provided I knew Megan's very existence had been a miracle.

I went to the office. I dumped the filter full of coffee grounds J.J. had left in the coffee maker, cleaned the pot—again—and set up a fresh brew. Fortified with a mug of black coffee, I settled at my desk and reviewed the contents of the envelope. What I had was a lot of information with little sense of the woman I would be tracking. My Internet search wanted to know if I meant Megan Mellquist. Megan Melquist with one "l" had virtually zero web presence—no images, none of the stuff I would expect from a thirty-two-year-old. I found one surprising tidbit. In our local weekly's Best of Santa Cruz edition, Megan had won the bronze for Best Bartender in the year 2000. That was pretty impressive. There were a lot of bars in Santa Cruz. It helped, I suppose, that she worked at a popular one.

I glanced at the time on the computer screen and added three hours. A guy in Jersey might be home from a regular nine to five job. I looked at the notes again. The ex was named Tom.

For a moment, my eyes did a dance between my purse and the desk—cell phone or office phone? I chose the comfortable—and I told myself, more reliable—landline. A woman with a heavy nasal Jersey accent answered. I flipped through the notes, but I didn't remember the wife's name because it was not listed.

I identified myself as Carol Sabala, and asked to speak with Tom.

"Carol Sabala," she said. "We don't know any Carol Sabala."

"I'm a private investigator."

"A private investigator?" Her voice was full of Jersey.

"I've been hired to find Megan Melquist."

"Oh, her. No wonder there's a private investigator." She bellowed, "Tooommm!"

A baby fussed, and I heard the woman say, "Honey, be careful, or you will spill that wooder." I guessed that was water.

The woman bellowed again. "I don't know. Some private investigator looking for Megan."

"Hello." The voice was manly and brusque and blissfully free of Jersey.

I identified myself and reiterated that I'd been hired to find Megan.

"Megan and I have been divorced for six years," he said impatiently.

"You were together for six years before that."

"So?"

He did not seem curious about what had happened to Megan—why a private investigator would be looking for her. I glanced at the notes. An insurance underwriter. I imagined him taking off his tie—harried—the wife and two kids downstairs waiting for him.

"You know her well, and I hoped you might help me get a better sense of her."

"Good luck with that." He had the deep, sexy voice of a disc jockey. "Six years, and apparently I had no idea what she wanted."

Bitterness. So she had divorced him.

"Well, you were both young," I said gently.

"Yeah, but I knew what I wanted." Defensive.

To be an insurance underwriter? "At the time, that included Megan, right?"

"She was beautiful. Smart. Rich." His voice relaxed like he had slipped off his shoes and sat down. "What was there not to like?"

"You tell me."

He sighed. "Me—all I ever wanted was a decent job, a good wife, a cold beer. Know what I mean?"

"And Megan?"

"I don't know."

After six years, he couldn't answer this simple question. Poor guy. It was clear she had dumped him. "You don't know why she left the marriage?"

"I think she was bored. Like you said, we were young. Megan was eighteen when we met, and nineteen when we got married. I think the idea was exciting to her, but then being married wasn't."

"So Megan liked excitement?"

"She was a searcher."

I let that sit, then asked, "What do you mean?"

"Hell, I don't know. She wanted to find the meaning of life, or something. She was just one of those restless literary types. Whatever it is she wanted didn't include me."

"Literary types?"

"A lit. major."

"There was no other guy or anything like that?"

Tom guffawed. "Nah. Megan's not like that."

"Innocent?"

There was a moment of silence. "Not really."

"How old were you when you met?"

"Why do you want to know that?"

"Just curious."

"Twenty-four."

I heard his wife bellow again. Up the stairs, I imagined.

"I have to go."

"Thank you. You've been most helpful."

Tom Melquist, insurance adjuster in New Jersey, actually had not been very helpful, but if needed, I wanted to be able to talk to him again.

I leaned back in my scruffy office chair, hands clasped behind my head, and conducted a post mortem of the conversation. The contents of the manila envelope painted the portrait of a girl who had been tall and awkward in high school. I speculated that she had gone off to college a virgin. The older Tom with the manly voice had swooped in. To a fresh-faced freshman he had no doubt seemed exciting. For a while.

A restless spirit, but loyal, Megan had stayed several years after the thrill was gone. Then she had shoved off to find a new adventure.

August, 1983

CHAPTER FIVE

The curves of her father's black Mercedes bent Megan's reflection like a carnival mirror. The image stretched even longer than her freakish five foot ten. She turned away and leaned against the car, waiting to ambush her father.

She was not going to give up this fight. She wanted to go to a big high school, the bigger the better, a place that might hold other misfits. She would not go back to her private school where all the girls were petite and perfect. And stupid.

Her parents just did not understand. They didn't know how it felt to be fourteen and tower over everyone. And to be growing! That was the scary part.

There was no hope arguing with Lucille. She just kept repeating. "I only want what's best for you." Megan tapped the car. Her father had pulled it out of the garage a half hour ago, but the metal was already hot from the sun. She swished her head back and forth thinking about how Madonna might sing her mother's refrain, *Only want what's best for you.* Her earrings hit against her cheek. Her black lace scarf shook loose and her blond hair tumbled down. She wanted to be wild like Madonna, to feel free, but whenever she looked into a mirror, she wanted to disappear—to be invisible. She wore the scarf and big cross earrings but no stack of bangles up her wrist, no lace gloves, no black lipstick. She wanted to. And she didn't. It was so confusing.

She stopped singing to herself. A part of her felt bad for ridiculing Lucille. The woman did want what was best for her. That was her mission in life, but Lucille's concern felt like a smothering blanket. She scratched at her bare arms. Her skin itched just thinking about Lucille.

Her father came out of the house, and Megan launched away from the car. Lucille was tall, but her father was six-foot-four and mostly to blame for her height. He looked perfectly groomed in his charcoal pinstriped suit with his black leather briefcase. From his appearance, you would never know Megan had been fighting with him all week, that this morning she had purposely dropped her breakfast plate on the tile, shattering ceramic and spraying scrambled egg.

Megan felt amped like she could take off running down the drive and run and run and never stop. She could run all the way to New York.

Her father glanced at her and jiggled the car keys in his hand. "There's my princess." He looked up at the sun, already glaring.

"Look at me, Daddy!" She sprang into his path. The big crosses hit against her cheek.

"You look beautiful."

Tears blurred her vision. "I do not. I'm a freak."

"Don't say that, honey." Beads of sweat formed on his forehead.

She blocked his way to the Mercedes. She knew he wanted to get to work, not because he had to—he was too important for that. He could do whatever he wanted. Right now, he wanted to get away.

"I want to go to a public school."

He heaved a sigh. "This has been decided." His voice held firm. He squatted down and scooped up her scarf from the slate driveway. "Your mother wants what is best for you." He held out the black lace like a peace offering.

She batted away his hand, the keys jingling. "I'm not Lucille's fucking science project!"

His jaw clenched. "Call her mom."

"No!" Since she was twelve, she had been calling her Lucille. She was not going to give up her one act of defiance.

Her father eyed his car. He jingled the keys hidden by her scarf. He glanced up again, his freshly shaven face pale in the bright sunshine. His gaze returned to her. "I'll take you to Six Flags."

Fury unleashed in her. He was trying to bribe her with their special thing as though it was nothing but a bargaining chip. The tears swelled in her eyes, and a drop trickled down her face. She swiped at it. "You are as bad as her. Just an old bully!" She emphasized "old" to pierce him, because he *was* old to be her father. He even had silver hair. He liked to pretend he was young, though, with his slut girlfriends. "I want to go to a normal school!"

"No," he said. "That's final."

"I hate you!" She lunged toward him.

He gasped, clutched the lapel of his Armani suit, dropped to his knees, and fell flat on his face.

She stopped short, squatted down and shook him. "Daddy!" He didn't move. Her eyelids blinked uncontrollably, and as she stood, the earth shook like they were having a quake. She ran into the house. She picked up the wall phone, but her hands trembled so badly she hit 9-1-2. She tried again. When the operator answered, she couldn't speak. Her favorite person in the world, and she had killed him. She dropped the phone, which bounced on its cord and banged against the wall.

Blinded by tears she rushed to the stairs. She tripped on the bottom step and crawled up the carpet.

"Mom!" she wailed.

NOVEMBER, 2001

CHAPTER SIX

With his Hawaiian shirt hanging open, Eric Mars stood in front of the flecked hotel mirror tightening and relaxing his abs. His green cat-like eyes flickered. He was one handsome dude. Men, women, old people, the young, all thought so. Even brown bitches like Brittany Bañuelos thought so, or she never would have lined him up with Megan. When he thought of Brittany, he imagined grabbing a fistful of her long hair, coiling it around his wrist and dragging her across the tile, her large breasts flopping as she yipped in *español*. He smiled at the thought and admired his straight white teeth.

He leaned in close to his reflection and fingered the sparse hair of the soul patch below his lip. He was just not meant to be hairy; this would have to do. On the plus side, women loved his smooth chest and ass. The thought of a hairy ass made him shudder.

Some of his looks had come from his mom. Once upon a

time she'd been a cute little free-love hippie. He didn't know who his dad was. From the vacuum of information, he figured she didn't know either. Someone tall.

With his hand curled around the neck of a Bucanero beer, he padded barefoot across his hotel room and stretched on the balcony lounger.

He hated this city. He hated the fumes from the old cars that drifted up from the Malecón. He hated that a person couldn't get a decent steak, or even chicken breast. It was all fish, drumsticks, and pulled pork, with propaganda billboards along the freeway proudly proclaiming Cubans ate Cuban pork. He'd figured that out without even knowing Spanish. What bullshit.

He sipped his not-quite-cold beer. The choices sucked—Cuban beer, light or dark.

He hated that no one on the street seemed to speak English unless they were girls sidling up to him and whispering like they got their lines from B movies, "Baby, you looking for fun?"

Even the black guys, snapping open their boxes of cigars, happy to take American dollars instead of CUC, became suddenly monolingual when he asked, "Cocaine?" Who would have thought in this sprawling, teeming dump he would not be able to buy drugs? But Havana was better than the hick town of Jagüey, where Megan had apparently shown his photo to everyone she encountered. Warning them like he was some kind of criminal. She was twisted.

He leaned back against the plastic straps of the lounger and closed his eyes, but anger at Megan roiled and the undersides of his eyelids felt itchy. He had thought she was the prize, another score like the Honus Wagner T206 white-rimmed tobacco card. Then she had deserted him and run off to Cuba! She had to pick some friggin' backwards communist country. She had no idea how much time and trouble she had caused him. And money. The banks and moneychangers screwed you for having American dollars.

He extracted a cigar and book of matches from the pocket of his shirt. He bit off the tip of the cigar and spat it on the concrete balcony. What kind of friggin' country didn't even sell Coca-Cola? And this "five-star" hotel room was crap. A joke. He'd stayed in better rooms at a Best Western.

Puffing the cigar, he smiled at the delicious irony. He was enjoying this fine tobacco because of a card jacked up in value by Honus Wagner's own anti-smoking campaign. Cigarette companies had issued cards like his to stiffen the packages, but the good old Pittsburgh shortstop did not want youngsters to purchase tobacco, and had his card recalled. As a result, the cards were rare and valuable, and at age twenty, Eric had made a small fortune on one. Now here he was smoking the best Cuban cigar money could buy.

A blapping noise penetrated his reverie. He sat up and leaned forward against the balcony rail. Below on the seawall, a man sat playing a trombone. That was a stupid ass instrument. Sounded like a tire going flat. It was giving him a headache. He leaned back and watched the blue smoke rise from his mouth like part of a magic act. Soon he would step through it, and Megan would see him appear.

Eric Mars puffed the cigar. *Megan, Megan, Megan.* He had come all the way to Cuba to take care of her. She thought she was dying. Well, there was no place she was supposed to die except in his arms.

CHAPTER SEVEN

I scanned the crowd in the San Francisco International Airport. They were mostly white, in their thirties and forties, couples. There was one Middle-Eastern-looking man, but like a lot of the passengers, in anticipation of Mexico, he already wore shorts. If a terrorist wanted a disguise, he should put on shorts. None of the young men I'd seen on the news, dancing on the American flag with rifles raised over their heads, wore shorts.

David looked more like a terrorist than any of the other people milling around the boarding gate. A nervous traveler by nature, David was examining the waiting room with his intense dark eyes. His olive skin was slightly sweaty. He hadn't shaved. At any minute, I expected security to crook a finger at him.

My presence at his side probably saved him from that result. Although I hated shopping, I had found a set of glorified sweats for the trip that were flattering and stylish. A bit of Spandex snuggled the black cotton to my form and the top was trimmed with black and white polka-dotted material at the cuffs, pockets and inside the hood. It was cute if I had to say so myself, but I didn't. David had nodded, asked me to turn around, and pronounced, "Very nice."

David was flying with me as far as Los Angeles, and his stratagem to overcome my objection had been brilliant. He had simply announced, "I'm going down to see Abraham."

He knew I would bend over backwards to help him repair his relationship with his son. If he were ready to fly to Southern California to see Abraham, I would do nothing to discourage it, like suggesting that he book a different flight.

Even though I hid my anxiety better than David, I was plenty nervous about my case—theoretically a person could be jailed for an illegal trip to Cuba. But I'd met with a friend of a friend of my boss J.J. who had assured me such trips were common. He had traveled to Cuba a half dozen times with no hassle. He had also established a contact for me in Havana, a guy named Alonso Rivas.

"The Cuban government may hate the United States," he told me, "but they're eager to have American tourist dollars."

Rather than put an incriminating stamp in one's passport, the country supplied Americans with special travel visas. The real dilemma would come on my return if a U.S. Customs Officer asked me if I had been there. Lying to Customs could draw a harsher sentence than the illegal travel. My leg bounced with nervous energy.

David laid his San Francisco Chronicle on one of the hard plastic airport chairs and patted my knee. "It's going to be alright. This is not the type of flight terrorists would be interested in."

David had misread me, but as was often the case, he understood me better than I did. Forget about the travel to Cuba, I felt jittery getting on a plane, and I felt glad now to have his company. "How is this so different than United 93 coming home from New Jersey?"

"That flight was headed near a target. Mexico is not a target."

"Well, before we get to Mexico, we have to leave here, and San Francisco is a target or we wouldn't have the extra security on the Golden Gate Bridge. Plus we'll be stopping in L.A."

I watched a young Hispanic male wearing earphones and leaning against the wall.

Instead of doing his job and reassuring me, David said, "Yeah, like we're really safer because people like us can't carry on razors and fingernail files. They should allow people like us to carry guns."

"How would anyone know which people are the ones like us?"

"Expert profilers. Like they use in Israel."

The airline began the special needs boarding. An old man with a cane hobbled toward the flight attendant. He was joined by an overweight, frazzled middle-aged woman in a foot cast, and a young couple with a baby.

"You know what I'd do if there was a terrorist on our flight?" David asked.

"This is not helpful."

"I'd take my fanny pack with my water bottle in it and hurl it at his face."

I agreed that would hurt. David had filled the bottle as soon as we'd gone through security. I watched the first class passengers file on.

When the flight attendant called our rows, the young Hispanic man pushed off the wall and joined us in line. He looked like a high school student in his black hoody and baggy pants. His head bobbed slightly to the secret world of his music.

David and I sat aisle to aisle so we could extend our legs and get up without crawling over people. The young man stood beside me and pointed at the window seat. Once folded into the tiny space, he shut off his CD player and unplugged himself for the take off.

"Good tunes?" I pointed at the CD player.

"Yeah. A buddy of mine burned it for me as a send off—all my favorite songs."

"Send off to where?"

"Okinawa."

"You've already done your training?"

"Camp Pendleton."

"A marine," I stated.

"Yes, sir," he said proudly, even though I was a lady. Or, a woman, at least.

I couldn't get much luckier than to be sitting by a combat-ready soldier. "Did you have a good send off?"

He grinned. "All-nighter."

He stripped off his sweatshirt, balled it up, and made a pillow in the corner. A puffy Semper Fi tattooed his bicep. He instantly fell asleep, his mouth open, so I was free to inspect his brown fade haircut and his unlined face.

As a redheaded flight attendant ran through the usual instructions, the people on board actually sat erect and listened. At the end of the spiel, she cleared her throat. "How many of you are flying for the first time since 9/11?"

David and I raised our hands along with the majority of the passengers.

"We are all so busy and live our lives at such a fast pace, but now we are here, together. Why not take some time to get to know one another?" She suggested that we turn to our neighbor on either side and introduce ourselves.

David swiveled toward me, his face scrunched. "Isn't this what they do in evangelical churches?"

I waved him away and angled toward the marine. Like an animal, he had lurched up at the departure from routine. I summarized what had happened and introduced myself.

His name was James—Jimmy.

"Pretty tired from the big night?"

He grinned. "Yeah. I partied with my homies and my

girlfriend." He dug into his baggies, extracted a wallet and flipped it open. A photograph showed the marine in a tux with a pink bowtie and cummerbund cuddled close to an Hispanic girl in a glittery spaghetti-strapped pink gown. Her honey-brown hair piled on top her head and spilled down rosy cheeks.

I peered closer at the gold-stamped *Love in Paradise, May 26, 2001.*

"You just graduated?"

"Yes, ma'am. In June."

I think I preferred *sir*. "How does your mom feel about all this?"

In the way of reply, he flipped to the next photo and showed me an impossibly young woman, seated, with her four children grouped around her, a studio shot, lots of red as though taken for Christmas. No hubby.

"She's proud," he said. "Happy I didn't choose the thug life like my dad."

If those were the options, maybe his enlistment was a relief. What a different world than that of Lucille Barnhart's privilege. Her wealth was as strange and intriguing to me as Cuba.

The marine told me about each of his siblings.

I felt glad that he was shipping out to Okinawa where he would be safe. For now.

He stretched, yawned, apologized for going on, put away the wallet, and groaned.

"I drank a bunch of Boston tea or something like that."

"They didn't card you?"

He pointed at the brand on his bicep. "Here's my ID."

He fluffed his hoody pillow, excused himself to catch some z's, rested his head, and without any fidgeting, fell back to sleep. His right hand curled under his chin and his left hand tucked in his lap. The next time I looked he was sleeping like a baby.

CHAPTER EIGHT

The plane touched down smoothly in Los Angeles and cruised along the tarmac toward the terminal.

"It's not too late to call it quits," David said. "You could come and visit Abraham with me." He didn't want me to go to Cuba, and he would welcome me as a buffer with Abraham. But, he was joking. He knew I wouldn't do it.

"My biggest worry," I replied, "is what I will say if an alert Custom's official notices I have two passport stamps into Mexico and no exit stamp between the dates."

"Your biggest worry isn't that I'll run off with a Southern California beach bunny?"

I smiled thinly, but my anxiety was as stubborn as the rest of me. "Do you think I should go for stupid and innocent. 'Geez, I don't know, officer'?"

David shook his head. "You just do not project innocent and stupid. I'd go with a story: The Mexican official stamped it first with the wrong date and then fixed it. Or, I took a bus into Guatemala, and for some reason they didn't stamp my passport."

I considered his suggestions. "I think I'll go with, 'I want a lawyer.'"

We both favored the latter. I was a terrible liar.

The plane slowed to a crawl. Stuffing books and phones into their purses and briefcases, passengers twisted in their seats, waiting for the ding to give them permission to unfasten their seatbelts. The young marine stared intently out his window. I jacked myself up in my seat and could see the ground crew surrounded by a gaseous haze waving the plane to its chute. The seat reclaimed my butt and I turned back to David with a flutter in my stomach.

He leaned across the aisle toward me. "The government really doesn't care enough about a trip to Cuba to engage in a lawsuit."

The flight attendant opened the door. We both jumped up to deplane as usual, but hung back, allowing other deplaning passengers to exit as if to forestall our separation.

I let the marine squeeze by me and wished him good luck. When several rows of empty space opened between the door and us, and the passengers behind us kept hesitating before passing us, we decided to move.

David walked me to my gate. Neither of us were the syrupy type, and Abraham would be waiting for him. He leaned over and kissed me. "I love you."

"Back at you."

"Be safe."

Watching him trundle down the wide polished corridor thronged with people, I felt relieved, but empty. In spite of the thunks of luggage wheels, and travelers broadcasting their every move on cell phones, without David's chatter my world seemed surrounded by silence. I was alone inside a bubble. I wished him back and at that moment he spun around. I blew him a kiss. He smiled.

Shortly after, I boarded the new jet headed from Los Angeles to Cancun. There was no allusion to 9/11. Maybe, as David had suggested, no one felt a plane destined for Cancun would be a target. Two young women completed my row—both blonde and blessedly thin. They were also speaking in French, which gave me an easy out just to smile and then to ignore them.

Once in the air, I concentrated on what lay before me. Alonso Rivas, my one possible Cuban contact, worked in a developing tourist industry. After the official collapse of the Soviet Union a decade ago, Cuba had fallen into a period of economic distress called The Special Period, which had led to the loosening of state control and the beginning of private industry. One new industry was the renting out of rooms in private houses—*casas particulares.*

Traveling on Lucille's dime, I'd thought at first to book myself into a five-star hotel in Havana. But it would be better, for the purpose of my investigation, to rub shoulders with regular Cubans, not newly arrived tourists from South America. Gus, the friend of a friend of J.J.'s, had Alonso reserve a room for me in a *casa particular.* I planned to carry one small bag, but he pressed me to take a few items for Alonso—a bottle of Tums, a wrench, and a Timex watch.

"Really, there is nothing to worry about," Gus had said.

A statement that never failed to make me worry.

As for my mission to locate Megan Melquist, Lucille had provided a regular dossier complete with an ample supply of color images printed from her computer. Megan had been a thirty-two-year-old woman with flawless skin, long dark blonde hair, and lively green eyes. After chemo, she became a hairless woman with a sallow face bloated from steroids. The eyes took on the look of a fierce, trapped animal. Strangely, Lucille Barnhart had also included a Polaroid of Megan as a preemie baby, a photo of her as a girl with missing front teeth, and a picture of her as a pretty, but gangly teenager.

When I had met Brittany Bañuelos at Starbucks, she had supplied me with three additional photographs—the first with a backdrop of red lounge leather. Megan snuggled back against a man's shoulder. Both Megan and the man looked shiny and blurry eyed.

Brittany pressed her finger against the man's face. "Eric Mars."

"Good looking guy." I sipped my black coffee.

Over one of those desserts masquerading as coffee, Brittany raised a thick eyebrow. "Very. He attracted people like double fudge brownies."

"So why did you set him up with Megan?"

"You mean as opposed to making a play for him?" Brittany licked at a whipped cream mustache. "He's not my type."

"In what way?"

She lifted her hands, both palms toward me. "I had no idea what an asshole he was. I just don't go for white bread. No offense."

"I'm half-Mexican." To her incredulous expression, I explained, "I look like my mom."

She shrugged, sighed and handed me the second picture. The couple stood on the sand of Seacliff Beach, with Eric clutching Megan's hand. Standing, Megan was a tall glass of water, as tall as Eric Mars. The sea breeze whipped her hair, and blew her gossamer sundress, revealing long pale legs. Behind them the Pacific stretched calm and bright blue.

"Eric is smooth. He gives off an aura of wealth."

"How so?" I asked.

She wiggled her fingers around her head. "Always groomed like he saw a barber every couple of weeks. Casual but expensive clothes."

I raised a brow. That didn't seem like much.

She leaned across the coffee shop table and whispered, "He made monthly deposits at the bank." She looked around the coffee shop to make sure no one was within earshot. "Not a payroll check."

"What kind of check?"

She pressed her index finger to clamped lips and shook her head.

I waited.

"I could get fired for sharing that kind of information."

I felt insulted that Brittany thought I would betray a source. At the same time, her reservation about sharing confidential information reinforced my opinion of her as a stand-up person. "Not personal checks?"

She shook her head.

Trust fund? Dividend payments? "Why didn't he make direct deposits?"

She shrugged. "Why don't a lot of people? They're lonely. They like the free coffee. They come in to flirt with the tellers."

"In Eric's case?"

"I think he enjoyed having the check in his hand. And the tellers flirted with him. He definitely seemed available and like a good match for Megan."

"Because they both were well-off?"

Brittany shrugged again. "Maybe something like that. They both seemed to belong to this other race, like aliens deposited here or something. Didn't Fitzgerald say that the rich are different than other people?"

"Fitzgerald, huh?"

She smiled grimly. "Yeah, well, there's a college major for my job; it's called English lit."

A sense of humor, too. I liked this Brittany Bañuelos.

She sipped her beverage, then leveled her eyes at me. "Megan was never a snob, though. Her mom wanted to send her to private school, but she insisted on public school. Harbor High. That's where we met. In English class. We were the two kids actually reading the books instead of running out to buy Cliffs Notes."

"Lucille never mentioned Eric."

"Lucille loves the guy—thought he was a saint for staying with Megan after her diagnosis. I saw Lucille and Eric together once, and she was practically giddy around him. Fawning. Like if he weren't Megan's boyfriend, she'd like to bed him herself." Brittany's full lips puckered in distaste.

Lucille as a type of Mrs. Robinson was not an image I could conjure. I believed she'd had sex in her life only because some event had produced Megan. The image of Lucille with her hair down and her pearls off was disturbing. I shook it away.

"You know," Brittany continued, "I think Eric's the one who tipped off Lucille that Megan was gone. And she probably blabbed to him about everything she found out."

"Interesting." I jotted notes. "Let's go back. Why did you feel Megan needed to be set up?"

Brittany sat up straighter and crossed her arms over her chest. "Megan is awkward around guys. She was already six feet tall in high school. Since I'm short, people called us The Odd Couple. Megan never got it that she could be a model, she just felt like a freak of nature. Me, I have six brothers. Half the time, I feel like another guy. Anyway, that shyness didn't magically disappear because the guys finally had their growth spurts."

Awkward and shy—a perfect match for an 'asshole' guy.

Brittany's thoughts must have been running down a similar stream because she said, "You have no idea how much I regret hooking them up." She pushed aside her half empty mug.

"I can't see someone shy making a trip to Cuba on her own."

Brittany waved away the idea. "She was shy, not timid, if you know what I mean."

"Not really." I considered the description. It sort of explained Megan's Best Bartender bronze award. In a crowded bar, no one was looking for a person to lend an ear, but, on the other hand, she couldn't be afraid. She would have to mix drinks quickly and competently for all sorts of people. No doubt her striking appearance helped people remember her later when casting ballots. She certainly didn't promote herself via social media.

"Megan loved the edge," Brittany said. "I think that's why she fell for Eric. And vice versa. She didn't know how to start a conversation with a man, but she would try anything. As for the travel, Megan's parents took her all over the world—Turkey and Indonesia and Africa. She's fluent in French. She doesn't have any fear about stuff like that."

My quarry—Megan Elizabeth Melquist—was flushing out into a complex character—not some hapless victim.

"French?"

"Yeah," Brittany smiled. "I used to kid her about that. Why not Spanish—something useful in California."

"Megan doesn't speak Spanish?"

"A little—the kind you pick up from living in California."

I pushed the third photograph back to Brittany across the coffee shop table. It showed Brittany's birthday party, a bouquet of balloons partly obscuring the couple, with Megan leaning back, arms crossed over an ivory-colored cashmere sweater, and Eric braced in front of her, a hand planted against the wall by her face, caging her, his pelvis thrust against her hip.

Brittany glanced down at the image and bit her lip. "I know," she murmured. She raised her flushed face. "In retrospect, it's easy to see he's an animal."

On the plane, the two women beside me had bent their heads together. If Megan were on the plane, would she seize this opportunity to speak French, or would she be too shy? Was she shy only with men? I wondered a lot of things. Had she been a Daddy's Girl, and when had her father died? I spent a few seconds chastising myself for not doing enough background research, and then forgave myself because another person's life was infinite, and never actually knowable. Questions would always remain. Still, I should have found out about the dad.

I pulled out my *Lonely Planet* for Cuba, and the young

woman beside me pointed at it with a big smile and held up the book in her lap—the same guidebook in French. Now that I knew the two were bound for Cuba, they became much more interesting to me. Their English was limited, but they nicely filled in each other's gaps, and I learned their primary reason for visiting Cuba (now that they had seen the over hyped Disneyland) were the "seg-zy" men. Perhaps they hadn't read the section about Cuban prostitutes and gigolos, another burgeoning tourist industry.

The two women were Swiss, from the Lausanne, French-speaking part of the country. Ingrid worked for a software company and Briget was her personal trainer. I didn't have much in common with them, but I was comforted when we reached Cancun, and they boarded the Cubana Airlines flight to Havana with me. Ducking my head, I climbed aboard. The Soviet jet was so old that one set of Cyrillic lettering was translated to Stewardess rather than Flight Attendant.

My assignment was in a two-seat row. I could easily reach out and touch the three-seat rows on the other side. Stuffing my shoulder-strap bag under the seat in front of me, I buckled up. My rolling suitcase that I could normally carry on had been stowed below. Crewmembers of an Italian airliner, hitching a ride to Havana, sat behind me in their reassuring dark blue tailored uniforms.

The flight attendant made her way down the narrow aisle and stopped, hovering over my shoulder. "Please take off your seatbelt," she said in Spanish.

I looked at her. Surely I had misunderstood, but she mimed unbuckling. The man at the window beside me didn't look up from his Spanish language newspaper. His seatbelt already draped down the side of the frayed cushion.

"*¿Por qué?*" This did not make sense.

"*Esta peligroso.*"

Peligroso—dangerous—was a word I'd learned early in Spanish along with *cerveza* and *donde esta el baño*. Even though

I'd had a Mexican father, he had not been around long enough for me to learn any Spanish from him, one of the many things I held against him.

The Italian pilot leaned forward and spoke in my ear in English. "They will refuel the plane now." He seemed unruffled. "It's below you."

Holy shit. With people aboard? I unbuckled and stood, although if the fuel tank below me exploded, neither action would make a difference. Brittany Bañuelos had told me: *We're all dying*. True that. There was no other way out of life. But I didn't want my exit to be here and now, even if the death would be sudden and exotic. I would prefer a fiery explosion to Megan's slow chewing cancer, but no death would be better.

When we were airborne and I was still alive, the flight attendant rattled down the aisle with her cart offering complimentary cups of rum. I needed a drink. I held the plastic cup aloft, and silently toasted the adventure before me. "*Hola, Cuba.*"

CHAPTER NINE

Eric Mars used the taxi ride to Catedral de San Cristóbal de La Habana to relish what he was going to do and how he was going to do it.

When he arrived at the square, the cab driver pointed at Eric's open Hawaiian shirt and then at the cathedral, a baroque, European-looking structure with two towers, one fatter than the other. The driver made buttoning gestures.

"No problemo," Eric Mars said. "I'm not going in the fuckin' church." As he paid, he noticed that the driver wore a gold cross around his neck. "Sorry, dude," Eric said, even though he didn't feel an ounce of contrition and the driver didn't seem to understand him, anyway. It was just Eric's habit to smooth over whatever he had ruffled. Stir it up and tamp it down. He was a master.

He turned his attention to the cobblestoned square, hazy in humid sunlight. An ocean breeze ran up his arm leaving goose bumps. It puffed the short sleeve of his shirt and flapped the front, making the hula dancers move. He'd expected a Caribbean country to be warmer.

He scanned the square. It pulsed with entrepreneurial spirit, Cubans ready to separate tourists from their Cuban convertible pesos. Out in the center, an old man dressed like a clown had a mutt sidekick dressed in a pink tutu dancing on its hind legs. Women dressed as gypsies had stationed themselves at each corner. They wore ruffled full-length dresses, their hair wrapped up in scarves. The younger ones carried baskets of fake flowers, but the older ones sat at tables and had big cigars in their mouths.

Eric sauntered up to the closest one—an older one—maybe fifty. Women were easiest. He had a way with them. He thought of Lucille Barnhart and smirked at her big phony wall of propriety.

The gypsy studied him and smiled with big red lips. She bent forward to give him an eyeful of the cleavage behind a bright blue ruffle. She cupped a deck of tarot cards in her hand and rapped them on the table, her bracelets jingling. "Would you like to know what the future holds for you?" she asked in careful English.

"Nah." He winked. "I know what the future holds for me." He gave her his best smile, a winning smile he'd been told. Did she really speak English, or only the lines she recited day after day to the thickening crowd of tourists?

"A photo with me?" she inquired.

"You are very beautiful," Eric said, "but no camera." He shrugged and lifted his palms.

The woman lowered thick eyelashes. Old, but fuckable, Eric thought.

"A kiss?" she asked.

He checked out her left hand. No wedding ring. No white telltale skin.

Without waiting for an answer, she rose and smashed her

lips firmly against his cheek as if to make a perfect lip stamp.

Behind Eric a collection of tourists clapped. He turned and sized them up. They almost looked American, but none of them were fat. Canadian, he decided.

"One CUC," the gypsy lady said.

Eric smiled even though a convertible dollar for a kiss was outrageous. And he hadn't asked for it, either. He gave her five CUC.

"Do you want to take photos with her?" Eric asked the Canadians.

"No, mate. Thanks."

"Would you take some of me?" Eric asked.

The tall, skinny head of the tribe with the digital camera around his neck looked perplexed, but like a true Canadian said, "Sure."

He snapped several photos of Eric as he looped his arm around the woman's shoulder, pulled her against his body. She smiled broadly, and her back muscles loosened up a bit. Sometimes these older broads had too much mileage on their Mohawk odometers, and it took more lubrication.

He touched the dark hair trailing down from the red scarf wrapped around her head. "How do you say hair?"

"*Pelo*."

"Beautiful *pelo*," he said.

After a few more photographs, the rest of the Canadians dispersed across the square, and the cameraman glanced after them. But he stayed, waiting to see what Eric wanted. "Would you like me to e-mail these to you?" he asked.

Eric Mars shook his head and busied himself with playfully counting money into the woman's outstretched palm. He laughed as the confused Canadian hurried off toward his group.

Photo op over, the woman promptly sat behind her desk, all business.

Eric Mars forced a smile. "*Pelo* salon?"

"You want hair?" With finger scissors, she made clipping

motions on top of her head. "¿*Barbaro*?"

Eric shook his head. "No. Hair salon."

"You have wife?" In spite of long red acrylic nails, the woman expertly shuffled her tarot cards. She peeked up at Eric through her lashes.

He shook his head. The woman finally seemed to be warming up to him for real.

"Girlfriend?"

He flipped open the wallet. Why not? He showed the woman the picture of him and Megan in the Red Room.

"Pretty."

"Have you ever seen her?" Eric asked.

"No."

The woman looked around now at milling tourists. She was a quick old coot, and he'd overstepped.

He tapped the picture. "She wants to get her hair cut."

The woman rapped the deck of cards on the table and peered past him for new customers.

Eric stood there, occupying her business space.

She sighed and picked up a pen from the table. Eric pulled the photo from his wallet and she wrote an address on the back.

"Ring the bell," she said, her English crisp and perfect. She narrowed her eyes up at Eric. "When someone appears, tell them Alvina sent you."

Eric bent down and whispered in her ear.

Without looking at him, she added another number and her price, fifty CUC for an hour.

"Do you have a car?" Eric asked.

"I can get one."

CHAPTER TEN

Instead of a state-approved taxi, I eyed a Yank Tank for the twenty-kilometer ride from the airport into Havana. The tall handsome driver lounged against the door hopefully watching. I nodded and held up my hand to indicate that I was interested. The odds of making a helpful connection seemed better with someone already operating outside the rules and regulations of Cuba.

Ingrid and Briget, my new best friends from Switzerland, stood with me on the sidewalk. We had bonded when the jet landed and smoke poured from the floor. "It's normal on old Russian jets," Ingrid tried to reassure me from several seats back. "Something to do with the air conditioning, I think."

In the dismal, unadorned concrete of the terminal, they nudged me into a curtained booth, where a stone-faced woman in a glassed-in cubicle thumbed through my passport, and then commanded me in Spanish to look up. I half expected cyanide gas pellets to release, but instead a camera snapped my mug shot.

"They want to make certain the person who enters the country is the one who leaves," Ingrid explained as we walked out into soft tropical air. It was almost dusk, but still I'd expected it to be warmer.

I asked Ingrid and Briget if they wanted to split cab fare, but they were bound for Viñales, which lay in the other direction.

"Gorgeous mountain climbers," Briget explained.

I remembered from somewhere that Megan liked climbing, wondered if she might have ventured to Viñales. Before we separated, I showed them the photos of Megan and asked them to try to contact me if they saw her. "A friend traveling down there," was the explanation I offered.

Briget pulled off her zip-up sweatshirt, revealing serious biceps. She didn't seem chilled by the breeze. We exchanged info.

"My cell number," Ingrid said.

"I didn't bring mine. My service is no good here." After years of resisting the evil, I had finally decided (with J.J.'s insistence that I couldn't be a private eye without one) to purchase a cell phone. Now here I was working a case where it would do me no good.

Ingrid shrugged. "Regular Cubans do not have them, either. They have *cellacracy* here." She smiled at her cleverness—in a foreign language, no less. "We will be at Casa Home Sweet Home."

Briget pointed her chin at the 1956 Chevy I'd picked. "Will you take that truly?"

"Yeah. I'm too stingy to accept the airport exchange rate for all my pesos." I'd brought a lot of Mexican cash with me, because tourists had to change their money into Cuban convertible pesos (CUC) and any currency received a better exchange rate than American dollars. Even though it was

Lucille's dime, I cared. With a gypsy cab, I could probably pay with foreign currency.

"Stingy?" Briget frowned with force. Even her face seemed muscular.

I nodded at my Yank Tank. "I prefer the risk of an illegal cab to getting screwed."

"Pardon?" she asked. "Screwed?"

I shook my head, fatigued with trying to communicate. Ingrid, whose English seemed more sophisticated, explained to Briget while I went off to negotiate my fare. Ingrid and Briget toodled their fingers at me and called out, "Ciao" as they headed in the opposite direction. I felt very alone.

The driver was a slender man with slicked back hair and too much cologne. He was eager to have my fare and agreed to take pesos.

"Don't get caught," I said to him in Spanish.

"No problem," he replied in English. "Do not worry."

But I did worry as he launched into the quickly descending night, the right front tire rotating unevenly. If we were caught, I wouldn't be fined or hauled to jail, but I would be asked to get out of the car, and I would be left there, wherever there was. I found myself slouching down in the hard bench seat.

"Where are you from?" he asked.

"California."

"Welcome to Cuba." He twisted back toward me with a big grin. There was no rearview mirror. "If you need a guide, I can show you around."

I felt wary. According to my guidebook the new tourist industry had brought along some of its less desirable elements. There were no MacDonald's or Starbucks, but industries like prostitution had gotten a head start. My driver's tight clothing made me wonder if he sold more than car rides. I dismissed the idea. His form fitting slacks and tailored shirt fit the stereotype that Cubans liked to dress. After all, they'd given us the Cuban heel for men. The cologne, however, was a definite luxury item.

I couldn't escape the stifling fragrance because both back windows were stuck shut.

"Do you need air?"

"*Sí.*"

"No problem." He opened his front window and a blast of toxic exhaust hit my face. I scooted as far as I could to the other side.

"Your English is very good."

"Thank you." Again he swiveled to look at me. "Do not worry about me." He raised his thick eyebrows. "I am a biologist."

Gus, the friend of the friend of J.J.'s, had told me not to be surprised to find doctors waiting on tables, or in this case, a biologist driving a taxi. In jobs where they might earn tips from tourists, Cubans could earn more than in their profession with government-controlled salaries.

My driver looked ahead at the mostly empty freeway and then twisted around toward me again. "Cuba is a beautiful country, yes?"

"Lovely," I muttered. So far, I'd seen the industrial airport and choked on the fumes from the old cars on the freeway. It was already too dark to view much of the landscape.

"This is my card. If you need a ride."

The information had been stamped onto plain white card stock in purple ink. He was Oscar Fuentes, Taxi and Tour Guide.

As we neared Havana, Oscar turned on the headlights of his car. They barely lit the highway. Not even the film of Buena Vista Social Club had prepared me for Havana's darkness. In the movie, the lack of street lights and the water splashing over the Malecón had seemed mysterious, and tempered with the music, almost romantic, but the reality of Old Havana was spooky. Scarred buildings reared up from narrow, rutted streets. Shadowy people threaded their way along narrow sidewalks.

My driver stopped in front of a tall building towering up

from a crumbling sidewalk. He pointed at a battered brown colonial-style door. At ground level, the building had no windows.

"This is it?" My throat was so tight I could hardly swallow.

He flicked on the car's lights again and indicated a tiled plaque on the wall. "2-2-4."

Shaking, I climbed from the security of the dangerous car, hitching up my shoulder-strap pack. Oscar climbed out, too, perhaps meaning to unload my luggage, but I pulled the carry-on bag from the seat. I crossed the street and tugged on one of the massive doors. It was locked. People passed by me—almost brushing my shoulders.

"Are you sure this is the right place?"

"It's a *casa particular.*" He pointed at a sign the size of a shoebox affixed to the stucco below the address. It featured a symbol that looked like an anchor. Oscar stepped up to the door, pushed a buzzer and backed across the street to peer up at the balconies. I followed suit. A figure appeared, silhouetted by dim light, on the top floor four stories up.

"I'm Carol Sabala," I shouted. "I have a reservation. Casa Maria?"

"Yes," he called back.

Later I learned that was the extent of his English. Now he buzzed me in, and I pushed open one of the two-ton doors over a large flattened cardboard box that served as a doormat. In the foyer a dim bulb dangled from a wire and another exposed wire ran to the doorbell along a salmon colored wall streaked from spilled items and rain.

Surely this was *not* where I was booked for the duration of my stay in Havana. There was not a single piece of furniture in the entrance, just a marble staircase with cracked and broken steps leading into darkness. I peered out at the street and hoped that running back to Oscar's car would be an option. However, his taxi, spewing exhaust, was already shaking its way down the cobblestones. Strangers slipped by, lit in the ambient light of the foyer and flats overhead.

I lugged my suitcase up the grim staircase, cursing Gus, the friend of a friend of J.J.'s, and his Cuban connection Alonso Rivas. I expected to crunch crack vials under my black athletic shoes, but now that I thought about it, in spite of the grubbiness of the street and the building, I hadn't seen a single bit of garbage—not at the airport, or along the freeway, or on the city streets. Maybe litterers got their hands cut off. By the time I reached the fourth floor, I was out of breath. I rang the bell for the flat. A deadbolt slid, a lock tumbled, and the door opened on my new home.

The man from the balcony stood there. I started the explanation of my reservation made by Alonso.

"*Sí,*" he said, surprised, and pointed to himself.

"You are Alonso?"

"Alonso, yes."

"And you made a reservation for me?" I asked in Spanish. I hadn't known the Cuban connection was going to book me into his house. But by this point, I wasn't surprised.

"Yes, yes, reservation," he said. "*Bienvenida.*" Welcome. He gestured me into a modest but reassuring living room, with a maroon doily-covered couch, and a couple of rattan rockers aimed at an old television set. French doors were open to the balcony and mild air wafted into the flat. The tile was so old the pattern had worn into a mottled gray, but the place seemed clean.

I was relieved at the room and relieved to be meeting a somewhat known quantity. Then he asked to keep my passport.

I looked at him again and thought about what Oscar, the taxi driver had told me—that the government was everywhere. Alonso couldn't look more average if he tried. He was the kind of guy no one would be able to select confidently from a police six-pack—about five foot ten, not fat or skinny. Although the majority of Cubans described themselves as mixed race, Alonso was fair with tightly curled light brown hair and an open, intelligent face lacking guile. "It's routine," he said in Spanish. He explained in the slow clear Spanish of someone used to dealing with tourists. He had to register every visitor as soon as possible, which would probably be before I was awake in the morning.

Government offices in Cuba must keep different hours than government offices in the States.

He gestured for me to follow him and we turned into a dining area, the space consumed by a long solid table and a sideboard. He pointed at a safe under the sideboard. "I will put it there."

I reluctantly handed him my passport, glad that I had a copy tucked safely in my bag.

I unzipped my single bag. "*Tengo regalos para usted.*" I have presents for you.

Alonso raised his eyebrows. "For me?"

I pulled out the Tums and handed them to him.

He looked dumbfounded at the box. "*¿Para mi?*" For me?

Maybe Gus, the friend of a friend of J.J.'s, had been wrong about what to bring for Alonso, and he was as bewildered at receiving a gift of Tums as an American would be.

I pulled out the watch and wrench, hoping they would make up for the faux pas Tums, but as I nudged them to him, he looked just as mystified. Gus, I explained, had sent these items.

The dawn of comprehension lit his face. With a sad smile, he regretfully pushed the items into my hands and launched into rapid-fire Spanish.

"*Despacio, por favor,*" I said, asking him to speak slowly, as I juggled the box of Tums, wrench and Timex.

He patted his chest. "Alonso Padura." He pointed emphatically at the gifts. "Alonso Rivas."

"*¿Hay dos Alonsos?*" There are two Alonsos?

He smiled and replied, "There are many Alonsos."

I was returning the gifts to my suitcase when a stout

woman in black skirt and blouse emerged from a dark side hallway. Alonso introduced her as his mother Maria. She welcomed me with a big smile on her face. She lifted her hands and made an outline of my body. "*Muy delgada. Elegante.*"

The "very slim" I accepted with gratitude since I was carrying five extra pounds of menopausal weight, but the "elegant" I rejected as pure flattery. No one looked elegant after a day of hard travel. My cute tracksuit was rumpled and I smelled of exhaust fumes and rum.

Maria offered to show me my room. We walked straight ahead from the dining room to the world's smallest kitchen, filled mainly by a large concrete sink and a tiny gas stove. She bent down to a hotel-room-sized refrigerator, opened the door, and gestured to large bottles of water. She flashed the gold work around her teeth and said, "Free." We continued into a short hallway with a door on either side. She unlocked the door into a tiny dingy room with two single beds. The room extended past the hallway with a window opening into an airshaft.

"*¿Hay un baño?*" Is there a bathroom?

Maria stepped inside and closed the door behind us, and beaming, waved her arm toward the step-up bathroom tucked behind the door. It was compact and everything looked new, but a second door led back to the hallway.

"*¿Es privado?*" Is it private?

She stepped up and demonstrated pushing the button to lock the hallway door, in case I'd never seen such a device. That didn't exactly answer my question, but I didn't want to come across like the Ugly American and decided it would do.

Left alone in my new digs, I washed up and laid down on the bed furthest from the door. It was hard and lumpy. I tried the other. It was so flabby I could feel the poke of the springs, but it wasn't quite as lumpy. I regretted not using Lucille's money for a good hotel. The investigator in me had thought I might learn more mixing with the natives than hanging out with a bunch of tourists. But, if I couldn't get any sleep, I wouldn't be much of an investigator.

I pulled the flabby mattress onto the floor space between the two beds. The springs underneath were rusty with age. I stripped the covers and sheets. Pulling the blankets from the lumpy mattress, I remade my bed on the floor using them as added cushioning. I lay down to test the results. Manageable.

Hearing a thump inside my bathroom, I sprang up. I pulled on the door, but it was locked. "Just a minute," said a pleasant female voice. After the flush of the toilet, I stepped into the hall where I met a silver-haired man waiting for the nattily dressed woman who stepped out of *my* bathroom. They were in the room across the hall with the double bed, had been in Havana for a week (using *this* bathroom), but would be off to Trinidad early in the morning. "Do you know that Trinidad is the oldest colonial city in the western hemisphere?" the man asked me.

I was glad that *my* bathroom would be returned to its private status by the time I woke up, at least until Alonso's family received its next guest, but I was also sad that this spry English-speaking couple wasn't going to be around.

Returning to my mattress, I propped on my elbow. I thought about Brittany's concern that Eric had not been to the bank since soon after Megan's disappearance. When he came in, he had tried using his charm to learn her whereabouts. Even if Eric was a classical abusive boyfriend, the idea he had followed Megan to Cuba seemed extreme.

I spread out the reports from the San Francisco private detective firm. Megan had flown into Havana five days before 9/11. Had she stayed in Havana or moved to the village where one could obtain the blue scorpion venom—for free—two days a week? Even though the San Francisco business never intended to send a private investigator to Cuba, it had racked up billable hours by gathering information about the miracle cure. A single family, whose daughter's pancreatic cancer had been miraculously cured by the venom, aka Escozul, had, in turn, devoted itself to breeding Rhopalurus junceus, a scorpion species endemic to Cuba. Now desperate people flocked to their house from all over the world. Tomorrow I would be one of them.

CHAPTER ELEVEN

Eric Mars strolled the cobblestoned Mercaderes Street, wandering over a block to Plaza de Armas. There could be a cherry on top of this shit pile of Cuba. Flea-market-like vendors occupied the perimeter of this square. Eric passed by the racks of ancient magazines, copies of old editions by Hemingway, and books written in Spanish, to a stall featuring cameras and watches and two manual typewriters.

He leaned across a scratched, glass-topped display case containing an array of knives. Those could be useful.

"Baseball cards?" he asked the proprietor, a wrinkly old guy in polyester pants.

The guy shook his head, seeming to understand. It must have been the magic word, baseball. He pointed a knobby finger across the plaza to another stall. A vendor trundled by them with a load of books on a dolly. The wheels were only metal rims. Eric glared down at the piercing squeak. This country was pathetic.

Eric cut across the square to the indicated stall. This vendor displayed a variety of stuff dating back to the fifties. He imagined that people left behind a lot of possessions when they fled Cuba during the revolution. He felt a stirring of excitement. When he was twenty-two, he'd bought a baseball card collection from a clueless young couple at the Santa Cruz Flea Market, a hundred bucks for the box. It had belonged to the girl's grandfather, and just like those stories you think you'll only read about, the lovingly maintained cards contained a Honus Wagner cigarette card. He'd sold the card for an even one million dollars, invested in stock, and built a cushion, but what he'd enjoyed the most was his mother's complete baffled incomprehension that he'd made money on a baseball card.

The dividends weren't enough to cover his lifestyle, but they allowed him to enjoy his work as a picker without sweating about constant scores. His expert eyes scanned the stall. Disney figures and a collection of American comic books from Archie to Superman. A near mint Little Lulu glinted with promise. He knew a collector who might take it.

At that exact moment the vendor approached, as though he could intuit a spark of interest. He was good, Eric Mars thought.

"Baseball cards?" Cubans loved the sport. In his head, Eric started to run down the professional players from the island, but the list was too long, probably pushing two hundred, including Jose Canseco—a great player even if he did juice. While he was here, Eric thought, maybe he could track down Cuban baseball cards containing rare examples of Negro League legends like Martin Dihigo, Jose Mendez, and Ray Dandridge.

The young guy nodded. He stooped down and pawed through a box—not a good sign. He held out to Eric a rubber-banded deck of cards, the edges frayed. None of them could be in better than fair condition. Still, Eric flipped through the bundle. This was his job, an occupation that appealed to women—the whole idea that he could scan the debris, the ordinary, the overvalued and spot the true underappreciated gems—well what did that say when he selected a woman from the heap.

He handed the worn cards back to the man. All the cards were of Cuban players he didn't recognize, ones who had never defected or become legendary enough to transcend the island. He purchased the comic book for the equivalent of a quarter.

"Does anyone else here sell baseball cards?"

The young guy shook his head, but Eric glanced at the other stalls before returning to the Mercaderes. At the corner of Obispo Street, he saw mimes ready to perform in front of a five-story pink building. They didn't have any real costumes, just old suits. One of the dudes wore three different plaids. They remained so motionless that Eric started to think they were not performers, but statues, and he and the gathering group of tourists had been doubly duped. Then the four guys began subtle, lizard movements—an eye roll, a dip of a hat.... Eric smiled at their deception.

He glanced at the structure—Hotel Ambos Mundos—and filed it in his mind. He needed a new place to stay.

"They have a National Circus School here," a woman said to him, as though he would be interested. He was used to women striking up conversations with him, although this one was middle-aged and had a big nose. Not good looking. And with her body...you couldn't even put a bag over her head. She had a maple-leaf flag pinned on the strap of her pack, but she might have put it there so people would not think she was a capitalist American. One of those imperialists who had invaded Afghanistan.

"This place was a famous Hemingway haunt," she continued.

He walked away from her. This cross street, Obispo, was cobbled and traffic-free for tourists, so he strolled down a couple of blocks. A Hemingway haunt. That would appeal to Megan.

Inspired by the mimes, he popped into a clothing store

and purchased a cotton guayabera, a shirt he would normally not be caught dead in. This one was really faggy with both embroidery and pleats running up the front. But the loose fit and big pockets would be great for hiding shit. He looped back to Mercaderes Street. As the afternoon drifted into dusk, he stopped at a joint where a band was playing songs from Buena Vista Social Club. He sat at a polished wood bar and ordered a mojito. A dark Cuban woman in a low-cut, clinging red dress with a flared skirt stepped in front of the band to dance, and Eric greedily took in the muscled calves in black stilettos, the skirt swinging from her hips to reveal flashes of black panties. The drink was stiff and refreshing, so he ordered another.

By the time he left the bar, night had descended, and he buttoned his Hawaiian shirt against the chill. Then he put on the guayabera over it. Why not? It would be warmer and he wouldn't have to carry a stupid bag. He rolled the comic book and stuffed the bottom into one of the deep pockets. The plastic bag floated off like a jellyfish. He walked another block to where Mercaderes dead-ended into Plaza Vieja. There were street lights here and primitive scaffolds lined some of the old buildings. A couple of the structures gleamed with fresh paint and people sat at white plastic tables out on the square. It looked like the government was trying to fix up this spot. When Eric crossed the open area and turned the corner, he knew he'd left the tourist zone.

Some guy on the plane had told him Havana was a safe city with little gun violence (and apparently no drugs) but that was probably if you stayed where you were supposed to, and you weren't Eric Mars.

The neighborhood he entered was even darker than the rest of Havana. The people weaving past him were dark, too, purer descendants of the sugar cane slaves. It seemed to Eric that blackness and poverty went hand in hand no matter where he went. But he felt buoyant as though a die were rolling to his number.

He threaded his way along the uneven sidewalk of Sol

Street, which sounded like Soul Street, which was funny enough, but the word meant sun, which was funnier yet. Eric snorted. A couple of young women dressed all in white ambled arm in arm in the street, their bracelets jingling, their voices squawking. He kept seeing girls dressed in white like that—a weird fashion in a dirty city.

"Hey!" he said.

The two girls spun around, their eyes big.

"What's with the white clothes?"

They stared and tittered.

He approached them and pointed at their clothing. One of the girls reached out and gently pushed his finger down. She raised her chin and put back her shoulders. "Santeria."

"*Gracias.*"

He watched the teenaged girls swish their way down the street. *Wasn't Santeria some kind of voodoo shit?* They looked normal enough.

After another block, he heard unmistakable metal clinks and human grunts emanating from an open double door. Inside, the building loomed cavernous and dark. As his eyes adjusted, Eric saw a fat bald white man with a cigar stub in the corner of his thick lips sitting at a small table with a cash box. The man glared inhospitably at him through squinty pig eyes.

Behind the man was a gym that reminded Eric of a prison yard. The floor was concrete slab, broken and worn in places down to the dirt. Rust flecked the free weights pumped by muscled, glistening black men.

Eric moved to step inside and another white man—also middle aged, but skinny—hurried over in his shiny red 1970s style tracksuit. A small white towel draped over his arm. "May I help you?"

"Can I work out here?"

The man looked him up and down, returned to the table and held a whispered conference with the boss. He hustled back to Eric.

"That is not possible."

"Why?"

The man stiffened. He crossed to the boss, and then back to Eric. "This gym is for Cubans only."

"I can pay."

The man shook his head and glanced nervously back at the boss, who pushed himself up from his folding metal chair and lumbered toward Eric. His heft carried the authority of power. The boss waved hammy hands at Eric and shouted something in Spanish that didn't seem very nice.

Eric stood calmly. This usually made people think twice. If he was so at ease, he must have a secret weapon, but that was his secret weapon. When the other person lost his temper, or her temper, and spluttered in frustration or anger, Eric arranged his face into a cool semblance of sincerity. He could feel when his lips were arranged in a hint of a smile and his eyelids hit the precise lift. He'd practiced it for years. It served him well. He didn't expect that to be any different in Cuba.

The fat man pressed close, spewing predictably. The skinny assistant put a hand between them like a referee. "You should leave," he said to Eric.

The dark interior had grown quiet. The shadowy black men had stopped lifting weights and turned their attention to the disturbance.

"I'll be back."

"That would not be a good idea," the skinny man told him.

Eric smiled at him. "I think it's an excellent idea." The clients looked like exactly the type he needed to talk to.

As Eric Mars sauntered out the door, he squinted at the stucco exterior, looking for a number, but he didn't see one. He counted the buildings to the cross street, even as he was already dismissing the idea of a gun. He thought of Megan's flawless soft skin. A gun was too impersonal.

And too messy. He didn't want to get his hands dirty—handfuls of evidence. However, if the police were as backward as the rest of the country, he didn't have to worry about forensics. Eric continued toward his destination.

After a few blocks, he found the address Alvina had given him. He pressed the buzzer and a young woman in yellow hot pants appeared on a lighted third floor balcony. "*Si?*"

"Alvina sent me."

The girl shouted back a stream of Spanish.

"Do you speak English?"

She disappeared through a sliding glass door and a tall white man appeared on the balcony. His hair was dyed a shocking red.

"Can I help you?"

"Alvina sent me."

"And what would you like?"

"A haircut."

"This is a beauty salon."

"Yes. I know." Belleza Bonanza. Although there was no sign anywhere.

The red-haired man shrugged elaborately. "I'll send down the key. Lock the door behind you." He ducked back into the salon. The hot pants girl with corn-rowed hair returned to the balcony and lowered a bucket attached to a rope. When it reached Eric's shoulder, he felt inside and found the key. It tumbled a deadbolt in a battered brown door, which opened into an empty foyer. He started up once beautiful marble steps. On the third floor, the hot pants girl opened the door for him, and he was in a small, too brightly lit room with a counter and three work stations, all of them occupied by women in various stages of having their hair done. One had straightened hair that the beautician was now shearing with a razor. Another had a headful of tinfoil squares. A third client's long lush tresses were being blown dry. Eric sat on a stiff backed wooden chair by the door to wait his turn, and scanned the racks of cosmetics for sale.

"Would you like a drink?"

The red-haired man indicated shelves of liquor bottles

behind the counter.

"Nah. I'm good."

The man ducked behind a curtain that separated the salon area from the rest of the flat. From behind the curtain, Eric heard the sounds of a woman cooing to a baby.

Eric's instinct said this was an illegal business. All the better. He wondered whether he should have his head shaved, or have his hair permed and dyed like the proprietor's. He contemplated the cosmetics and various shades of lipstick displayed on a glass shelf.

CHAPTER TWELVE

During a sleepless night, I flipped from one side to the other. Every time I rolled to my right, I smelled sewer. When I tried my left, I smelled propane. I vowed to change my accommodations the next morning.

However, in the morning, Maria, dressed in the same black skirt and blouse, stood in the kitchen like a personal butler awaiting the arrival of the great Carol Sabala. The matriarch gestured for me to sit at the long mahogany table and informed me that breakfast was included with the price of lodging. She lavished me with strong Cuban coffee, small bananas cut lengthwise and guava and pineapple slices. She whipped a towel from a tray of bread, indicated an array of jelly and honey, and told me I was beautiful and skinny. How would I like my eggs?

As I was loading the fresh bread with my scrambled eggs, the deadbolt clacked and the front door swished. Alonso entered the dining area, handed me my passport, and asked how long I would like to stay. I found myself saying that I would be there another night. "Then we'll see."

His guileless face smiled happily, and when I was ready to head out on the highway, he called the taxi driver/tour guide/ biologist Oscar Fuentes for me. Speaking Spanish on the telephone was twice as hard for me as speaking in person when I could read body language.

From the balcony, which might hold five chairs squeezed in side by side, I watched for Oscar's car. On the rooftops across the street, telephone wires and wash lines and antennae crisscrossed busy patchworks of corrugated metal held down with scavenged hunks of concrete. A shirtless young black man squatted on one of the roofs tending to a pigeon in a makeshift cote.

I returned my gaze to the street. Oscar's car came around the corner and rattled down the cobblestones. When the car disappeared below the balcony, Oscar blasted the horn.

I snatched up my backpack and ran down the three flights of steps. I shouldered open the massive, scraping door, locked up, and crossed the street to greet my fragrant escort. Even though I'd obligated myself to another night at this Casa Maria, I wasn't about to take a bus to Jagüey when I could use Lucille's money for my own personal English-speaking tour guide. I was anxious to see what kind of family would devote their lives to raising scorpions in order to dispense a free supposed cancer cure to the world.

"Jagüey," Oscar said with enthusiasm. "I know a good *casa particular* in Jagüey."

I hoped that I was not about to endure an hour-and-a-half sales pitch: I know a good restaurant. I know a good bar.

Our first order of business was a trip to Regla, one of Havana's municipalities on the other side of the Bay. Oscar pulled up to a small turquoise stucco house that sat right at the edge of the sidewalk. I took the wrench, Tums and Timex from my pack. The "real" Alonso wasn't home, but I was able to stuff the items into the hands of his friendly, startled, and joyous wife. She invited me in, but I indicated the waiting taxi. She gestured that he should come, too. Oscar sprang out of his car before I could protest.

The door opened into a small room. A red velvet settee ran along a wall with a coffee table in front of it. A Santeria altar occupied the corner. A cigar, a glass of rum, and a pink hibiscus had been offered up to a carved figure that wasn't Jesus or the black virgin or any saint I recognized. Oscar and I sat uncomfortably close together on the red settee as Yolanda, Alonso's wife, served us coffee and offered rum to enhance it, even though it was nine o'clock in the morning. Oscar reached for the bottle.

"You have to drive me to Jagüey," I protested.

"We will go soon," he said.

Was he not getting my drift or just pretending not to? I may have been in a foreign country, but some aggravations were exactly the same.

Once we left the slums skirting Havana, we hit a flat freeway in fairly good condition and without much traffic.

"That's because only twenty percent of Cubans have cars," Oscar explained. "See those people standing along the side? They're waiting for someone to pick them up. It's the law in Cuba that if you have a car, you have to pick up travelers."

Oscar, however, wasn't stopping.

"You see," he explained, "unless you have a way to get a car through the black market, the only cars that can be bought and sold in Cuba are the ones from before the revolution. Otherwise, you have to be connected." He sighed and shrugged.

"Aren't things starting to change?"

"Slowly. Very slowly."

The countryside rolled out, green and agricultural—pretty, but hardly breathtaking. As we neared Jagüey, the billboards increased. One depicted what looked like a ham topped with several steam pots and one-ring hot plates. *Con esfuerzo y consagración avanzaremos y venceremos,* which translated to something like, "With effort and dedication we will advance and win," but what exactly the people were supposed to win eluded me—a free ham, perhaps. Another depicted the Cuban flag and *Este es el partido de la patria.* This is the party of the country.

Oscar cleared his throat. "This part of Cuba is very…." He rubbed his angular nose and searched the blue sky for the word. "*Patriótico.*"

"Patriotic?"

"*Sí.* Fidel Castro occupied a sugar mill in Jagüey during the Bay of Pigs. He led the counterattack from there."

"Interesting."

Oscar brightened. "I can take you to the museum."

It would be fun to see Fidel's headquarters, but I had work to do. I shook my head, and reminded Oscar of the address.

We passed an overgrown sugarcane field with a schoolyard across the street. One house past the field, Oscar swerved up to the sidewalk. After the decaying structures of Old Havana, the one-story cream-colored house before us appeared solid and in good repair. A faded red bicycle with a wooden seat was propped in front of the small yard where a tropical accent tree offered some shade. A few people waited outside the door. The first three in line all looked Cuban and were squeezed together on an iron bench. Behind them, stood an elegant woman in a flowered dress and red straw sunhat, who obviously belonged with the chauffeured black Mercedes-Benz parked in front of Oscar's car.

Across the street a group of skinny boys played baseball on the bare lot at the back of the school. Home plate, a scuff in the dirt, was near the fence. The pitcher launched a green tennis ball and the batter swung a stick, grounding toward first, and both teams erupted into excited cries. I sat for a moment. I enjoyed their play and resourcefulness, the fun they managed without proper equipment or uniforms. American parents would be shocked how little was required.

"He's out," Oscar said. "He didn't have a chance unless the first baseman bobbled the ball."

I smiled, glad that Oscar had a source of entertainment for his wait. I joined the end of the line and asked the well-dressed woman in Spanish if she were waiting to see Señor Duarte to receive Escozul, the official name for blue scorpion venom.

"Escozul," she said, nodding her head, and I realized she didn't speak Spanish and probably had not understood anything else except the name Duarte.

"Do you speak English?"

"Little," she said.

"Where are you from?"

"France."

Could this stylish woman with glossy hair be a cancer victim? Since I didn't speak French, I wouldn't learn much from her. How she planned to communicate with Señor Duarte was one of life's little mysteries.

"*Con permiso*," I said in Spanish, taking a step around her toward the people on the bench.

She scowled.

"I just want to talk to these people."

The two men and the woman on the bench looked up at me.

The French woman turned toward the street and aggressively beckoned with her bejeweled hand. The red nails glinted in the sun.

Her chauffeur, dressed formally in maroon livery, climbed from the Mercedes. Oscar had already sprung from his blue and white Chevy. Even though a Rumble in the Jungle between two chauffeurs seemed imminent, my attention was drawn to a tall man across the street. Smoking a cigar, he leaned in an overly casual way against a telephone pole. When I looked his way, he swiveled toward the baseball game. His bald head shone in the sun.

Oscar and the chauffeur didn't square off or bark at each other. Instead they greeted each other with open arms and big smiles. They clapped each other on the shoulders, and exchanged a few words.

Friends? Fellow biologists?

When they entered the yard, the French woman spoke to her driver, slicing the air with her hands and pointing a painted fingernail at me. Her driver spoke to Oscar in Spanish. I grasped the situation and the driver's Spanish before Oscar asked me in English, "Are you trying to move to the front of the line?"

I could understand how someone might want to as the line had yet to move. When it did, I doubted it would be quick. I explained that I just wanted to talk to the three waiting patrons in front of the woman.

Oscar, in turn, explained all this to the chauffeur, emphasizing that I understood my place was *after* the French woman. The chauffeur relayed this information to the woman, who stood stiffly. Large white-framed sunglasses hid her eyes.

Oscar spoke in rapid fire Spanish to the chauffeur. They both grinned and strutted toward their automobiles. For a while, they leaned against the Mercedes, chatting and watching the game across the street.

Cigar in his mouth, the bald man pushed away from the telephone pole, sauntered across the street, and took a place behind the French woman. A razor nick on his pate indicated his head had been shaved, while the soul patch he sported looked artificially black, almost like he'd taken shoe polish to it. Wearing black horn-rimmed glasses and a pale yellow guayabera, the man looked like a jazz musician. He also looked oddly familiar. He angled away from the line, as if not to disturb us with his smoke.

"*Buenos días*," I greeted the three Cubans seated on the iron bench.

They'd been watching all the action and waiting in

anticipation. All three smiled and greeted me.

The man at the head of the line had gnarled feet in beat-up huaraches and wore an ancient brown cowboy hat with holes in it. I soon learned the bicycle belonged to him. He had pedaled over from the next village.

"*Mire.*" He was telling me to look as he bent his head forward to show me a tumor protruding from the back of his neck, dark from years of stooping in the fields.

The thin woman next to him clutched a pink sweater around a yellow blouse as she relayed how she had hitchhiked from Havana. She had breast cancer that had been metastasizing at an alarming rate before she had begun to take Escozul. Now, after coming here for six months, she felt much better and the cancer had stopped spreading.

I understood her Spanish very well, but that was probably because of the context. I half knew her story before she spoke.

The third man, who was thin and as shiny black as ebony, regularly made the journey by bus from Trinidad to get the Escozul for his mother, who was too sick to travel.

"She can eat again," he said happily. "*Es un milagro.*" It's a miracle.

The door opened and a young woman greeted us all. From what I'd read, a single family operated this free distribution of scorpion venom. The young woman, with her rosy cheeks and thick, glossy hair, must be the daughter, the one who had survived the supposedly terminal cancer, making believers of them all. She motioned in the man with the neck tumor.

I moved forward with him, pulling the photos of Megan from my pack. "*Solamente quiero preguntarle a ella unas preguntas.*" He seemed okay with me asking the young woman a few questions, so I stepped in front of him, avoiding the eyes of the others in line.

The girl at the door looked me up and down. "Who are you?"

"Carol Sabala, private investigator." I handed her my card.

My sweetheart David would be proud of me. He'd worked hard to train me to have my cards at the ready. I'd even written the name of my *casa* and its number on the back.

"You are from the United States?" The girl's crisp English shamed my Spanish.

"Yes."

She nodded toward the old man, standing behind me, waiting to enter the house. "You told our client you wanted to ask me some questions?"

I fanned the photos for her to see.

"Have you seen this woman—Megan Melquist?"

"We don't discuss our patients."

"So she is your patient?"

I recognized the expression on the girl's face. I'd seen it a hundred times. The jaw muscles tightened so the mouth wouldn't open. She'd clammed up. J.J. and I often did legwork for a public defender who was fond of saying, "You can't catch a fish if it won't open its mouth." Fortunately for the world, most criminals were not as smart as a fish. Not that the girl was a criminal. Given the work she was doing, she was closer to a saint.

I tried, "Megan's mother hired me to find her, to see how she's doing."

Nothing.

Nonetheless I asked, "Will Megan be here today?"

The girl gestured for the man with the tumor to enter. My animal instinct sensed other people in line now staring at my back. I wasn't making any friends by pushing my way to the front and then holding up the line. Not wanting to block the old man's way, I stood aside. Once he crossed the threshold, the girl shut the door in my face.

I returned to quiz the two on the bench. The Duarte family dispensed the scorpion venom two days a week: Wednesday and Sunday. Since the Cubans had been coming to the make-shift clinic for a long time, chances were fair that they had seen

Megan. "Do you recognize this woman?"

The man from Trinidad shook his head, but the tiny woman from Havana nodded, and launched into a long story of hitchhiking from Havana and being picked up by this woman. However, by that point, she had already been on the outskirts of Jagüey. They had traveled together for about five miles. She didn't know much about Megan except that she came here to the Duarte house.

"Excuse me." The bald man had edged up to the group. He pointed his cigar stub at the photograph. "I know her."

CHAPTER THIRTEEN

Eric Mars' green eyes narrowed into slits as he regarded the new arrivals in the Chevy. The owner had tried to cherry the car, but the tires were worn and the body lowered, not on purpose, but because the springs were shot. He watched the woman crawl out of it. She wore athletic shoes, Levi's, sweatshirt, and he could tell she was American by the cadence of her English as she talked to her driver. He heard her say, "This might take all day." She had an assertive walk as she entered the yard and tried to worm her way forward in line. When the two drivers climbed from their cars, Eric crossed the street. He sensed conflict, and it reeled him forward.

His body snapped on to high alert, the hair on his arms raised and his blood throbbed. Eric had visited the house last week, and it had been clear that Megan had tipped off the family about him. He doubted now that Megan would return in person, although this seemed like the best way to trace her.

If she believed the cockamamie bullshit venom was helping her, she'd need someone to get it for her, and Megan didn't have the Spanish to talk some Cuban into doing it. This American woman had the earmarks of a possible courier.

As Eric approached, both drivers and the two standing women observed him as though they thought he might be coming to join their argument. With satisfaction, he noted their startled looks as he got closer and the way they quickly averted their eyes.

Eric stood at the end of the line, angled away from the others. On his previous visit to the house, Eric had learned that Megan must have shown the family his picture and told them all sorts of crap about him. The father and daughter had been on guard and didn't let him get a foot in the door. They wouldn't tell him a thing, even when he ramped up the charm. The girl yapped on about the confidentiality of medical records as if they were a real establishment—pure horseshit. They'd already been pulled into Megan's web. No doubt they had reported back to her that he had been around. He twisted his head and scrutinized the small crowd, wondering if any of them had met Megan and how much of her story they bought.

That was the problem—people believed Megan. It was that wispy, vulnerable act she had. Those long milky legs and the pretend shyness. The helpless way she could never get her life together, moving from wife to grad student to barista to bartender. It was fucking annoying. Even he'd fallen for her poor-me act. He'd believed her when she said she loved him and would never leave him. He squirmed, trying to get comfortable with the constraints of the decorative pillow belted under his shirt. This little trip of hers to Cuba had been a kick in the balls. Women didn't leave him. He left women.

Now she was talking shit about him when he had never done anything to Megan she didn't want—that she didn't ask for.

The thought of Megan made him itchy. He scratched the top of his head. He stopped abruptly because scratching looked nervous. He relit his cigar—what was left of it—drawing the rich, calming tobacco into his mouth and throat and chest. The drivers walked back to their vehicles, yakking away like old buddies. As Eric exhaled a plume of blue smoke, he turned toward the people in line. He didn't recognize any of them except the old guy in huaraches. On his previous visit, Eric had seen him pedaling away on his bike. Eric didn't worry. His disguise was brilliant. He especially loved the chewing gum stuck at the top and bottom of his gums, changing the shape of his face. He'd stolen the pillow from the hotel lobby and cinched it under his pants and shirt. In the mirror it looked ridiculous, like he was wearing a pillow, but people saw what they expected to see. They would see a man with a potbelly, not a man with a pillow in his pants. And that was if they bothered to take a good look. Most people would see the lipstick and turn away in discomfort as the group in the yard had.

He listened to the American woman sputtering in Spanish to the Cubans on the bench. She didn't say much, mostly listened to their sob stories. It seemed to him that when the natives spoke Spanish they made long faces and slathered on the tragic tone, trying to communicate their sorrow even to someone like him who didn't understand the language. The scene reminded him of a cartoon.

When the Duarte daughter finally came out of the door, he twisted away. The huarache guy with the hideous lump on his neck went up to the door and the American woman practically elbowed him out of the way.

Eric studied her. She didn't move like someone with cancer. She had sprung up from her squat like a jack-in-the-box. About five eight, her frame looked strong. Her face wasn't bloated from cortisone. When she showed the girl something, the American woman gesticulated energetically. On the other hand, her hair was really short, like it was growing out. If she did have cancer, it would have taken Megan about two minutes to convince her they were soul mates. Megan could have manipulated the woman to pick up the drug for her. Megan was a pro at getting what she wanted. Look at how she'd lured him all the way to this shithole. The only person who seemed to have the slightest clue about Megan was her mother, and Lucille was a piece of work herself—a complete control freak. Eric snorted. In spite of Lucille's properness, he could have porked her in a heartbeat.

The old guy went into the house, and the American woman crouched down by the two Cubans on the bench. She was showing them photos. Eric edged forward. The dressed-up woman in front of him stiffened and scowled at him. The two Cubans huddled together over the photos. The black guy slowly wagged his head, but the rat-nest hair on the scrawny little woman bobbed up and down.

"Pardon me," Eric said to the foreign-looking woman at the end of the line as he tried to step around her.

She whirled and almost sliced his forehead with her friggin' hat. He couldn't see her eyes behind the white-framed sunglasses, but Eric doubted the eyes were lighting up with the instant pleasure to which he was accustomed. His current disguise was meant to repel. He pointed at the photographs and stepped by her.

The American woman cast a wary glance up at him. Did a slight double take. Frowned. He smiled and inched closer. She turned back to the little lady, and asked her stuff in an excited Spanish.

Eric froze. The woman had photos of Megan with him. This American woman had not come as Megan's courier. She was searching for Megan. Since he was in the pictures, she must know about him. She couldn't be anyone official; the police in the United States did not consider Megan a missing person. Even the firm Lucille had hired had refused to send someone to Cuba. Lucille must have found someone new. However, Lucille could not have supplied the photos in the woman's hand. That had to be Brittany. The stupid bitch.

Eric's instant, intuitive alertness to danger melted into a sensual liquid that flowed through his body, a warm internal bath. His mother used to say he had a screw loose—when she was sober enough to notice anything. Mostly she lounged in front of the television while she drank Popov vodka and schemed how to get her next buck without actually working. In spite of her, he'd been popular, in the way girls liked hot-looking bad boys, and the way guys admired fearlessness. Want somebody to climb to the roof of the school? That would be Eric Mars. Jump off? That would be Eric Mars.

The skinny Cuban woman's bony hands sketched the air. He understood the words Habana. Auto. The woman's gestures. His best guess: Megan had once come from Havana in a car and picked up the Cuban woman. The story confirmed his belief that Megan stayed in Havana between pick-ups. He'd never really thought she stayed in this rinky-dink hellhole.

Havana was a big city, and this American woman, this investigator or whatever she was, equaled a lead plopping right down in front of him. Let her do the work and lead him right to Megan.

Eric stepped closer to the huddle.

"Excuse me," he said in English. With all the junk in his mouth, his voice was mumbly. He enjoyed the strange sound of it. He pointed at the photo. "I know her."

CHAPTER FOURTEEN

Megan leaned down to pay the government taxi driver. He raised caterpillar eyebrows in skepticism.

She understood. This area outside of Havana was even more rundown than central Havana, and unlike central Havana, it had never been well off to begin with. Many times, Megan had strolled up and down the tree-lined walkway in the middle of central Havana's broad boulevard, Paseo del Prado, seeing through the deteriorating facades to Havana's past of elegance and wealth. This area, though, had never been part of that Havana, the international nightspot full of mobbed-up casinos. Here, humble houses offered stucco walls, worn unevenly through layers of colors, until they resembled muted abstract paintings. The wall in front of her was a textured masterpiece of soft yellow, ochre, and peach.

This poor taxi driver had to wonder if she knew what she was doing. Possibly he knew the residence belonged to a babalao, a Voodoo high priest, or had deduced as much by her white blouse and skirt and necklace of red seeds. She didn't know what the necklace signified, but when she'd made her intent known in a Havana shop full of Santeria goods, the saleswoman had draped it around her neck.

She smiled down at the worried looking cabbie as she handed him the necessary CUC to pay him and to provide a generous tip. On the short ride, she had learned that his claim to speak English included things like, "One, two, three, four, five, six, seven, eight, nine, ten," and "First president George Washington!" all proudly exclaimed.

He seemed like a sweetheart to her. She pointed at a young woman standing at the edge of the road who held a sign that said, "Megan" as though this were a busy air terminal. The girl waved to her.

"Translator," she told the taxi driver to reassure him, although the woman hardly reassured her. In a pleated gray skirt and matching vest, the translator she'd hired for the meeting with the babalao looked like a schoolgirl. With light brown hair and fair skin, she stuck out in this neighborhood. The high priest, Megan had been told, could trace his roots to the Congo.

She waited for the cabbie to leave before she approached the translator, who greeted her in perky English. Megan couldn't remember her name and didn't ask. "Let me make it clear, again," Megan said, "that I want nothing but translation. I want the experience to be as authentic as possible."

"Certainly," the girl said.

Together they approached the door of the house. This High Priest belonged to the Palo Monte lineage of Santeria, or Voodoo. Possibly she was about to do something crazy, Megan thought, but frankly, she had no use for that word. *Crazy* caged a person in a box. It was crazy to stop her treatments. Crazy to come to Cuba. Crazy to drink scorpion venom. Yet, as she rapped on the door she felt stronger and less nauseous than she had felt for her last three months in the States.

When she'd first been diagnosed, she read a book *Love, Medicine & Miracles* by a doctor, a surgeon actually. He argued convincingly for the power of belief. Maybe the curative power of blue scorpion venom was all placebo effect, but if it worked, who cared? This visit could be the same. *What could it hurt?* She was already drinking poison and roaming around Cuba with an expired visitor's visa. With the expired visa she could no longer enjoy the comforts of Hotel Parque Central, but rather endured the discomfort of an illegal *casa particular*.

Colette Delvaux, whom she'd met in line for the venom, had recommended this high priest, Felipe Maldonado. He had changed Colette's life. He had given her the strength to support her husband through his cancer, to make the trips back and forth from France to Cuba. After seeing the high priest, "*J'etais pleine d'énergie*," Colette said. She'd been charged with energy. "*Ça m'a procuré un sentiment de puissance*." She had been given a feeling of power. The high priest Felipe Maldonado offered the protection of an orisha, a spirit manifestation of God. Right now, Megan had to admit, she could use some protection and power. Plus, Colette had added, Felipe Maldonado was a healer. She didn't say it, but Megan knew the woman was implying *in case the venom doesn't work for you*. Colette had chewed her lip, because as she had shared, for her husband, the venom had not been a cure, but offered only relief from pain. That alone made the voyages worthwhile.

Megan towered over the slender man who answered the door. He was shriveled as a ninety year old, and appeared a bit formal in slacks, hat, and long-sleeved, yoked white guayabera. She'd expected something more exotic—a robe, at least.

He greeted them in Spanish. The translator stepped up beside Megan and presumably explained her role because the old man spoke to Megan. The girl translated, capturing the same solemn tone, "I have a gift from God. I cannot sell it. I cannot give it away. I use it to do good for others."

"Okay," Megan said. She stood outside the door, not knowing how to respond to his speech. This wasn't an unusual feeling for her. She wondered sometimes if she might belong to a species other than Homo sapiens. She couldn't remember any natural bond or connection with people—not even her family—especially not her family. The closest she'd come to a "normal" relationship was with Brittany, and that had a lot more to do with Brittany than with her. The most connected she'd ever felt was with Eric Mars. That had to say something about her.

Fortunately, the man did not seem disturbed by her lack of response. He gazed up at her with dark raisin eyes that seemed to accept her as she was, and gestured for them to follow him.

He led them through the darkened living room, out to a yard strewn with rusted junk, and into a lean-to. The dim, humid confinement reeked of blood.

CHAPTER FIFTEEN

I stared at the strange man standing beside the bench in the yard of the clinic. He had just claimed to know Megan. This was too good—too easy—to be true. The man was over six feet tall and had broad shoulders, but it was hard to determine his age because up close I could see he wore make up. I had the vague feeling I'd seen him before.

I fanned out the photos and held them up to him. "You know her?"

"Well, I met her here when I came for my treatments." The man sounded like he had a mouthful of marbles. "We're both American, so we talked a bit. She was from Santa Cruz, in California."

I tried to tamp down my excitement. "Do you know if she is staying in Havana?"

"Yes, she is, as am I."

"Do you know where?"

"Alas, I cannot help you with that. I offered to share a ride here to pick up our Escozul, but she declined. She said that she would not be coming today. Perhaps she thought I had ulterior motives. She seemed like a shy young lady."

The guy knew enough about Megan that I was convinced he had met her.

"I gave her my number," he said, "in case she changed her mind."

"You have her number?" I almost yelped.

He shook his head. "Alas, no."

The line moved forward as the man with the tumor left the house and the skinny woman in the pink sweater entered the front door. Clutching a brown paper bag, the man hunched toward us. He stared up at us and halted in his tracks.

I wished the *campesino* good luck in Spanish. He smiled at me and nodded. He took another hard look at my weird new acquaintance before he continued to the sidewalk to retrieve his bike. He wrapped his bag from the clinic in an old towel and, using a short length of rope, strapped the package into a large wire mesh basket welded onto the back of the bicycle. He pedaled off.

I turned back to the man beside me. The French woman now hovered near us, probably to remind us that we belonged behind her in line. I inspected the guy. Make-up foundation colored his face a peachier shade than his tanned neck and pale naked scalp. Red lipstick had smeared off with wisps of color now outside his lip line giving him a clownish appearance. If he was trying to cover a cancer symptom, it was tough to imagine anything that could look worse than his make-up. Certainly he was not a transvestite. Transvestites knew more about make-up than most women.

He didn't have an obvious tumor like the man who'd left and he wasn't reed thin like the woman who'd entered the house. He appeared healthy.

"If Megan contacts you, would you let me know?" I asked.

"Yes, indeed."

Young lady? Alas? Indeed? The guy spoke as though from a past generation, or as though he'd been raised abroad. The speech did not match his body, which leaned over, straightened, and twisted with the ease and grace of a young person. Nothing fit together right.

"What's your name?" I asked.

"Aaron Phelps."

As Aaron Phelps took in my appearance, I had the disquieting sense that his green eyes were trying to hypnotize me, to suck me into a void.

"If Megan contacts me, how do I reach you?" he asked. "Where are you staying?"

CHAPTER SIXTEEN

Megan cleared her throat. She wasn't sure she could stomach the stench of death. Even though she'd started to experience good days, she still suffered bouts of nausea. Just a whiff of pine-scented cleaner, the odor of her chemo clinic, could make her vomit. But it was the translator who emitted a small gagging sound.

In front of a cloth-covered altar a candle flickered on the floor, casting shadowy ghosts on the walls. Felipe whipped away the cloth. Megan squinted through the dimness at the mound of fur and feathers—a dangling head, the glassy eyes aimed toward her. To confuse matters, a set of cow horns jutted, straddling the side of the altar.

"To please the orishas." The High Priest beamed at her as he spread his arms wide toward the dead goat and pigeon. "Today is a day with many visitors—a big day for healing."

His wrinkled hand swooped with the grace of a flamenco

dancer's to indicate she should sit in one of two chairs placed side-by-side facing the altar. The translator glanced at the other chair, but the old man indicated with a brusque gesture that it was not for her. He seemed unconcerned that she had to stand, which suited Megan perfectly. The girl took up a position behind Megan's seat. The high priest crossed the room to the wall formed by the stucco exterior of the house. He flipped a light switch. Nothing happened. Megan followed the old man's gaze up to a fluorescent light. A frayed cord dangled down from it to an outlet on the same wall.

The old man stuck his head out the door. "Huve! Marcos!" His orator's voice boomed the names. For a holy man he sounded plenty annoyed.

A young man sporting cornrows and gnawing a stick of sugar cane entered the room. Megan didn't know if he were Huve or Marcos, or what relation he bore to the babalao. A grandson maybe? The healer didn't introduce him. The young man scraped the empty chair across the floor until it was beneath the fluorescent light, clambered up, and wiggled the prongs of the cord more firmly into the light fixture. The bulb sputtered to life. The young man jumped down, returned the chair to its proper position, and left without once removing the sugar cane from his mouth.

The healer took his seat beside her.

"Let me explain why I'm here," Megan said.

Before the translator could speak, the holy man raised a hand—salmon-colored palm toward Megan. "No."

The babalao picked up some small stones from the table and tossed them back down like jacks. He arranged them into a pattern and uttered something.

The girl behind her immediately spoke. "You have a serious illness and you feel fear."

The man turned to Megan with shiny eyes.

Megan was unimpressed. That was a safe thing to say to any of his clients. People didn't come to sit in a hot room rank with the stench of dead animals because everything was hunky dory in their lives. Besides, she looked ill. With the scorpion venom and the simple Cuban diet, her complexion was regaining its pearly quality, but she was pale, and it didn't take a rocket scientist to discern there couldn't be much hair under her scarf. Her hair was sprouting back to life, but was coarse and curly, not like her hair at all.

Megan had to admit the translator was good, seamlessly relaying his words, "You have been crying."

She had, but not too much, and again that seemed more like a logical guess than a divine revelation. When her body had failed to respond to chemo, she thought nothing remained but tears. Lucille had barraged her with this new research and that new clinical trial. It had gotten to the point that she felt if she didn't keep trying western medicine, her mother would blame her for her own death. She'd had to escape.

"You are a quiet person," the healer said, "so people often fail to see you are a brave soul. You will try everything in your power to heal, and you will succeed."

These words startled her, seemed plucked from her very heart. Her eyes filmed with tears. Not even Brittany had supported her quest and the idea of alternative medicine, but here in Cuba, people embraced folk remedies. They validated her quest. She blinked and inhaled deeply. A mistake. She strangled on the odor and retched.

The old man sat, unperturbed, touching the objects. He didn't seem finished.

"But?" Megan asked.

He looked at her, puzzled, even though the translator had fed him the word. He waited for several seconds before responding. "This will not cure your pain."

Megan regarded the old man with alarm. She had come with a degree of skepticism, wanting to believe in the power of faith, but knowing this guy could be another huckster. However, the longer the session lasted, the more personal it became.

Maybe the babalao did have magical powers.

She knew precisely what pain he was referring to: The sun bearing down on her. Her father sprawled in the driveway. Her throat restricting.

The babalao spoke and startled her from the memory. The words floated down from the voice behind her. "Your life will still be in danger."

Megan blinked. Her stomach fluttered. The old man knew about the lingering threat to her life—a threat she might not ever escape. A threat that some days she wasn't sure she wanted to escape. Eric. She cleared her throat. "Can the orishas help me?"

The translator spoke, and the old man turned his salmon-colored palms up and lifted his hands, indicating Megan should stand. "Hold the horns."

Megan stood at the side of the altar and bent down to grasp the cow horns, which were placed wide apart. Her stance felt uncomfortable and vulnerable. For the first time, she glanced at the translator, who had remained behind the chair where Megan had been sitting. The girl clutched the plastic back. Her face was white and her eyes averted.

The scooped neck of Megan's white blouse dipped enough that she thought the old man might view her cleavage, and the heat of embarrassment crawled up her neck and face. Her time with Eric had left her aware of the erotic possibilities of this position, and she glanced over to make sure the little man didn't have any big ideas.

Seated in his chair, he stared at her like a teacher who had seen her eyeing another's test. He spoke to Megan, and the translator intoned, "Repeat these sentences after me in the language of your origin."

"Okay."

He rose. His first sentence was, "I, Megan Elizabeth Melquist, submit myself to your presence."

Megan almost lost her grip on the horns. She did not

remember giving the babalao her middle name. The idea that the old man communicated with a higher power frightened and exhilarated her.

Her throat clenched again against the stench of the room. She cleared it and repeated his sentence.

She followed him through an invocation of *Tierra Tiembla*—Shaking Earth—and the saint Las Mercedes. In call and response fashion they pleaded for wisdom and justice.

Megan's back ached from her awkward stance. The room was windowless and even in her lightweight garments, she felt sticky and damp under her armpits. Her hands slipped on the cow horns. She wished she had not swathed her head in the white scarf, but she got tired of people staring at her peach fuzz hair. She retched again and the acrid swill of vomit lodged in her esophagus. She willed herself not to puke during the ceremony. Half of what the priest asked her to say sounded like mumbo jumbo. She didn't think that was the fault of the girl, admirably earning her CUC in what must have been one of her more bizarre translation jobs. Megan repeated the words the best she could.

After several minutes, the high priest indicated she could return to her seat.

He sat beside her. How could he appear so cool in his polyester slacks and long-sleeved shirt?

"You are now the daughter of Obatala, the orisha of creation," he said solemnly. "Your color is white, representing all that is pure. The best foods for you are white—rice, custard, and milk."

Megan smiled slightly—not exactly the advice of American doctors. She'd even seen the dietary slogan, "If it's white, don't bite."

Felipe Maldonado, the high priest, then pointed a finger up at the faulty light, although Megan thought the gesture was supposed to be reverential, indicating the sky or universe. Or, maybe it was just supposed to signify the light.

"The Palo Monte religion is powerful," Felipe intoned. "We are in Cuba, in Colombia, in Venezuela, in Spain, in Miami, and in California! You are now part of the Tierra Tiembla branch of Palo Monte, daughter of Obatala! Go forth with courage."

He dropped his hands and turned toward her. His dark eyes grew sad. He picked up her hands and sandwiched them between his. "My daughter," he said, "be bold." He closed his eyes for a moment and then opened them slowly. "But be careful. Death is looking for you."

CHAPTER SEVENTEEN

I moved under the shade tree in the yard and wrote down the address and phone number of Casa Maria along with my name. I handed it to my new acquaintance, Aaron Phelps. A lead trumped the heebie-jeebies he gave me. If Megan contacted this guy, I could be well on my way to finding her. But something held me back from giving him my card.

He glanced at the info on the paper. "Old Havana?"

I nodded, surprised that he knew the city so well. "I might have to move someplace with a more comfortable bed." I bent my head side to side, cracking my neck. After a night on the mattress on the floor, my back felt like a slab of marble. "In case I move, how can I get in touch with you?"

He smiled. "Yes, Cuban beds leave a lot to be desired."

He lingered slightly on "beds" and "desired," so the simple statement gathered a sexual charge. I felt flustered, even though we weren't alone. The French woman was watching us, and the man from Trinidad rested on the bench near the front door, his long legs stretched out across the walkway. I mustered the driest response I could. "Yeah, as far as I can tell, the embargo just means ordinary Cubans can't get a new set of bedsprings."

"I will be moving as well." He glanced at my information again. "Carol Sabala."

My stomach flipped, and I suddenly wanted to snatch the piece of paper from Aaron Phelp's hand, but he continued smoothly, meeting my eyes. "There is a hotel in Old Havana—Hotel Ambos Mundos. Ask for me there."

The French woman had stepped so close to us that the musky fragrance of her perfume swirled around my nose.

"Excusez-moi." She pointed at the photos clutched in my hand and launched into a torrent of French. I glanced at Aaron, but he shook his head. He didn't understand French either. While she spoke, I envied her sunhat and big glasses. The temperature had been steadily rising, and the shade from the yard's tree had shrunk into a small ring. My former mane of hair used to be hot, but at least it had protected my scalp and neck from sunburn. Now as I listened, hoping to understand a single word, I felt my exposed skin crisping like strips of bacon.

"I don't speak French," I reminded her, pointing at her chauffeur. "We need your guy." I called to Oscar, who was sitting in his car with the door open. He seemed engrossed in the kids' game across the street, but turned when he heard his name. I gestured for Oscar to come, and he ambled toward us. The French woman called to her chauffeur. He strolled up the short walk in his shabby maroon livery, arriving with Oscar, the two men exchanging curious expressions. The woman spoke to her chauffeur.

While the woman talked, Aaron elbowed Oscar and nodded at the kids in the lot across the street. "You like baseball?"

Oscar shrugged. "I'm Cuban." He averted his eyes, possibly so as not to stare at Aaron's powdery make-up and lipstick.

I shifted my weight and shot them my best basilisk stare. Oscar should be paying attention while the woman spoke to her chauffeur, although as far as I knew, Oscar didn't understand any more French than I did. The overgrown tropical flora around the yard corralled us together. With our group of five and the guy waiting on the bench, the yard was crowded.

"How about Luis Tiant?" Aaron asked Oscar.

I scowled at them. Luis Tiant must have been a special ballplayer because Oscar raised his eyes. They shone with excitement. "The father or the son?"

I tapped Oscar's shoulder and indicated that he should listen to the chauffeur's report, but what the chauffeur provided in Spanish seemed like an abbreviated rendition of the woman's words. Cuban Spanish was fast, and the chauffeur wasn't trying to accommodate me, so I understood just enough to make my adrenaline sprint. This woman, too, recognized Megan. I guess I should not have been surprised. Cancer victims prepared to drink scorpion venom made for a select group of people.

"Does she know where Megan is staying?" I asked the chauffeur in Spanish.

He translated to the woman in French.

"Havana," she replied.

I didn't need help to understand the woman's disappointing response, but I glanced at Oscar, anyway. Left out of the loop, he was shuffling his feet and staring at Aaron, almost as if in a silent plea to resume their conversation about baseball and relieve the tedium, but Aaron watched us. The pale make-up accented his green eyes and his body had frozen like a stalking cat's. As soon as he saw me looking his way, Aaron turned. The guy gave me the creeps.

If the French woman knew Megan's specific hotel or *casa*, she would have given the name, because that was the way with people eager to help. Still, to make sure, in Spanish I asked the chauffeur if the French woman knew Megan's address. He translated and she shook her head. She had not moved me even one block closer to locating Megan.

I asked her name.

She understood without translation and said, "Colette Delvaux." She lowered her sunglasses and regarded me with lovely hazel eyes highlighted with two shades of taupe eye shadow and long, thickly mascaraed lashes.

"Carol Sabala," I offered.

We shook hands. Hers were slender and soft. Mine were stronger, but not nearly as elegant.

When Oscar heaved a weary sigh, Aaron turned to him, and asked if he had a business card. Oscar whipped one from his pocket and handed it to him. With a jerk of my head, I indicated to Oscar that we should talk in the car. As far as I was concerned, we were done here. I'd found out what I could, and according to Aaron, Megan Melquist was not coming to the clinic today.

When we started toward the Chevy, Aaron tootle-dooed his fingers, smiled at Oscar, and said, "Luis Tiant senior was a great lefty."

Oscar pointed his finger at Aaron. "You know your baseball."

Aaron winked.

CHAPTER EIGHTEEN

Eric imagined pressing his thumbs into her windpipe until she started to pass out. He'd show that aggressive American bitch a thing or two. She'd interrupted his conversation with the driver like he was a no-count, a worm. Eric Mars stuffed the primitive business card of Oscar Fuentes, Taxi and Tour Guide, into the pocket of his guayabera along with the piece of paper.

He extracted a fresh cigar. The sun was burning his newly shaved head, and he backed toward the trunk of the tree, moving into the small circle of shade. He ran the length of the fragrant tobacco below his nose. Cigars and baseball players, the only two good things about this God-forsaken island.

He resumed his fantasy. He'd choke her and then….What was her name? He fished the crumpled paper out of his pocket. Carol Sabala. He stuffed it back into the shirt. And then….He admired the long elegance of the Montecristo. Yes, that was an idea, except it would be a waste of a good cigar.

The French woman pointed at the Montecristo, said something to him, and waved a slender hand as if to fan away smoke.

He hadn't even lit the damn thing. "Angel," he said, "you have no fucking idea who you are dealing with."

Her shoulders rose as though maybe she understood "fucking." She spun away from him, arms crossed under her breasts, and heaved an injured sigh. Even though space had opened on the wrought iron bench, the woman didn't move forward to sit with the black man sprawled there. The man's head rested against the stucco house, and his eyes were closed.

Maybe he should have turned on the charm with Ms. Frenchy, but in his disguise, that was kind of hard. This woman knew something about Megan, but he couldn't extract it without French. Eric glanced toward the Chevy at the curb. Carol Sabala faced her driver, deep in conversation. Too bad she had suddenly become cautious before her driver translated everything. He chewed the tip of the cigar to give himself a tease of the enjoyment to come. Lucille must have hired this Carol Sabala woman to find Megan. That would be exactly like Megan's mother. The woman devoted her life to trying to control her little world. He smiled. People like Lucille didn't realize when they gripped so hard, they crushed everything. Control freaks were so fun to mess with. He bit off the tip of the cigar and spat it into a bush.

It was fine that Carol Sabala might have information that he didn't. Better even. She could do all the legwork, and he'd follow her right to Megan.

His gaze drifted to the French woman. Her flowered dress snuggled a trim waist and the bare arms bore a fleshy vestige of youth. Would her nipples be dark or pink? Probably dark because she was French, even though her skin was pale and the hair not covered by her enormous red hat was reddish. So maybe pink. He liked little rose buds like Megan's. He tried to concentrate on whether a French squeal would sound different, but he couldn't get into it. Megan had destroyed this part of his life, had castrated him. He pushed away from the tree and glared through the leaves at the white hazy ball of sun. The only way to regain his power was to destroy what had sapped it.

Stuffing the cigar into his pocket, Eric strolled to the front of the yard. He took a stubby pencil from his pants pocket and added the license plate numbers of the Mercedes and the Chevy to the paper with the name of the investigator and the address of her *casa particular*.

A man and a woman were shuffling past the deserted sugar cane field toward the house. Before they reached the yard, Eric returned to the tree, marking his place in line, even though he was two yards back from the French woman. The new people appeared to be a couple. She was clearly the sick one, her weight slumped against the shoulder of her short husband. They stood behind him, but the guy eyed the bench.

The skinny Cuban woman exited the house with a bag, and the black man wearily lifted himself from the bench. Holy shit, Eric thought, the guy was at least six foot five. The young woman he'd met before, the one that must be the daughter of the family, ushered in the guy, who stooped through the doorway. The French woman sat down on the empty, shaded bench, but Eric stayed back by the tree, reaching out to catch the departing Cuban woman by the shoulder. She was so scrawny he came up with just a fistful of pink sweater. Her beady eyes widened in surprise, but not anger. She hunched protectively over her paper bag.

"So you met Megan once?" he asked the old Cuban woman.

She shook her head.

"You didn't meet Megan?"

"No *ingles*."

He released the sweater. Just another thing he hated about this country—the number of people who didn't speak English. The place was so backward. Here in Jagüey he'd seen farmers shouting out stuff for sale—bananas, pineapples, cucumbers, bread—whatever, as their horses clomped down the streets pulling rickety carts. Forget about the Twenty-first Century. They hadn't even entered the Twentieth.

Eric waved his hand impatiently for the couple to move forward. "Go ahead."

They smiled at him, meek and submissive. He knew that they understood he was allowing them to pass forward to sit; he was not relinquishing his turn to enter the clinic. For now he would enjoy seeing how the French woman reacted when the guy parked his sick wife beside her. To his disappointment, she simply slid along the bench to make room.

He felt irritable in the gathering humidity. This was taking all day. Now that he had Lucille's search dog to find Megan, did he need to wait around here on the slim chance Megan might show up? With his altered appearance, he had hoped to pry some information out of the Duarte family when he got in the house. He didn't want all the trouble of the disguise to be for nothing. He ran his hand over his head and felt pricks of stubble. He took a deep breath. There was no trouble. The past was gone. The future didn't exist. There was only the present. Which was uncomfortable. He chafed under the restrictions of his disguise. If he were in his natural state, he could amuse himself, melt the French woman like a piece of wax. Instead, he sweated from the pillow in his pants.

Cuba constrained him like a straitjacket. How exactly was he going to sign into a hotel as Aaron Phelps when they would ask for his passport? In the States, with nice clothes, money, and maybe a white lie, he went any place he wanted. Here, he didn't know how to maneuver. He didn't know for sure what could land him in jail, what his rights were, or how much his American lawyer could do for him. Supposedly they had American detainees rotting away down here.

He would have loved to snort some coke and trash his hotel room, but he'd had to content himself with leaving a brown log floating in the toilet, a nice ambiguous present that they would never know was intentional.

CHAPTER NINETEEN

I cranked at the Chevy's window handle, but it stuck after a half rotation, a good metaphor for the way I felt. We'd baked in the car for a minute. Oscar hadn't offered me any information from the conversation with the chauffeur that I had not already gleaned.

"Stop," Oscar said. "That is all it will go. As I drive, it will get cooler."

"Back to Havana then."

"No Castro headquarters?"

"Not today."

The taxi fired a plume of black smoke. After having labored to open the window, I now tried to turn the handle to close it. The handle wouldn't move. The fumes drifted forward.

"You have to jiggle it."

The handle was locked in place.

"Not the handle, the glass."

The toxic smoke had already entered the cab, so I left the window cracked, hoping the car would air out. I glanced back at the yard. "That guy is weird."

"The cosmetics are strange." Oscar gripped the thin steering wheel. "But he likes baseball. He cannot be all bad."

I didn't reply. I was miffed that Oscar had given Aaron Phelps his business card. Now he was defending the guy.

As Oscar drove, I reminded myself that he wasn't David, my loyal pit-bull of a boyfriend, or even my flawed, aggravating boss, J.J. Sloan. Oscar was just a guy I had hired for the day to drive me around. He didn't owe me any allegiance and had every right to pursue future business. The problem was with me, not Oscar. I was cranky from difficult travel followed by too little sleep. I reminded myself that I was being paid well, and that supposedly I liked a challenge.

I'd already understood the heart of what the chauffeur had relayed to Oscar in Spanish. The French woman, Colette, who had flown all the way from Paris to get Escozul for her husband, met Megan at the Duarte house. Megan was a lovely young lady. How sad to have cancer at such a young age! Colette had gone on in that vein.

On the way back to Havana, though, I felt a niggly, the mental equivalent to the physical sensation of something unseen crawling on one's neck. Nigglies drove me crazy, because the harder I chased after them, the more elusive they became. They were the vibrations of my subconscious, which would work at its own pace, and there wasn't a damn thing I could do about it. I let my head fall back against the seat and admired the blue Caribbean sky, an occasional royal palm thrusting into my view and waving at me.

Halfway back to Havana, my stomach yowled like a cat in heat. At the first rumble, Oscar's slouch jerked upright. He observed me, but I kept my gaze up at the sky, following the drift of my thoughts. The second time, Oscar said, "Are you hungry?"

I was beyond hungry, probably another reason I felt tired and irritable. I'd stocked up on the fruit, bread and eggs at the *casa*, but that had been hours ago.

"Yes," I conceded. "Starving."

"I know a place."

Of course you do. I wondered if the "place" belonged to his cousin or if he got a kickback for delivering customers. The quick negativity, like my noisy stomach, signaled that I was out of fuel. The truth was I could use a connection down here in Cuba and Oscar was a potential candidate—my only candidate at the moment.

"Cuban food." His brown eyes peeked at me. They were large and thick-lashed. I could imagine a lot of women would find him handsome, but he was in his upper thirties—tops. To me, that was starting to seem like a kid.

"What else?" I was too famished to restrain all sarcasm.

Fortunately Oscar smiled. "Cuban food—for Cubans."

"Okay," I said, not sure what he meant, but intrigued by the mystery and too hungry to care.

When he arrived in Old Havana, he drove to an area spruced up for tourists. Down a rutted side street, he found a parking spot half up on the sidewalk. "*You* can't pay in this restaurant."

Maybe because my blood sugar had reached zero, it took me two full beats to grasp what he meant. I fished a bill worth twenty convertible units of currency from my pack. "Will this cover it?"

He smiled broadly. "That is more than adequate."

Did this arrangement mean I was also paying for his meal? To prevent awkwardness, I volunteered, "This is my treat."

He didn't protest. Instead he hopped out of his car and trotted around the front to open my door.

Oh, for crying out loud! My first impression of Oscar as a possible gigolo rushed back at me. I might have snatched back my twenty CUC bill if he hadn't already stuck it into his tight pants. Instead I gently pulled away from his proffered arm and said, "This is just a business lunch."

He smiled and held up an open palm. "Of course. Just business."

I squeezed my eyes shut for a second, and then stared directly into his big browns. "Just lunch." My diction was crisper than crostini.

He laughed, shrugged elaborately, and said, "Of course. Just lunch."

I followed him, feeling like an idiot. He turned onto the fixed-up cobblestone street, and we threaded through a touristy crowd. He entered a courtyard full of small round tables, some of them occupied even though it was well into the afternoon. Painted brick walls rose on both sides of the courtyard, and overhead a vine-laced arbor provided shade. It was a pretty, pleasant spot. It did not strike me as a Cuban restaurant for Cubans, but what did I know?

A white-aproned waiter greeted Oscar and ran his eyes over me as I trailed behind him. I stared right back at the guy and followed Oscar into the restaurant. The smell of fried fish filled the smoky air. My mouth salivated.

The interior dining area held four wooden tables. A very blonde couple occupied one. They watched us walk around the counter, past a cash register, and into the kitchen.

A cook stirring something in a big dented pot waved at Oscar. I recognized the aroma of beans. The cook turned his back to us and flipped two fish fillets that popped and sizzled when they met the grill. A kid twisted around from a single, deep concrete sink to look at us and whispered something to the cook. Laughing, the cook glanced over his shoulder at us and Oscar held up two fingers. "*Dos platos*."

We exited out the back of the galley kitchen into a fenced enclosure that contained a row of three metal garbage cans. One of the cans didn't have a lid and flies swarmed around the top. It reeked of dead fish. Oscar mimed holding his nose. As though I needed a prompt.

In five strides we were across the enclosure. Oscar stopped and rapped on a splintered wood door. A squat man with bare arms like ham hocks cracked it and Oscar whispered to him. The guy rose up on tiptoes to peer over Oscar's shoulder at me, opened the door and swept us inside.

This courtyard was bordered by the same painted tan brick and covered by a similar pleasant arbor, but the four white plastic tables were bunched together, so if they were occupied, people would be eating elbow to elbow. At the moment, though, all the tables were empty.

Oscar tried to pull out one of the plastic chairs for me, but I waved him off, still not certain he understood we were simply having lunch.

The man who bulged like a bouncer wedged through the doorway.

"I hope you don't mind that I ordered for us," Oscar said.

"What are we getting?"

"Fish with rice and beans. Real Cuban food."

"Great—as long as the fish is well done." I had a gag reflex to slime—raw oysters, egg whites, okra, and undercooked fish.

Oscar stood up. "Beer?"

I would have loved an ice-cold brew, but I shook my head. I needed to stay awake. "Bottled water would be great."

Oscar left. I heaved a sigh of relief. I imagined telling David about the experience when I returned to Santa Cruz. We'd have a good laugh. For a day or two, David would probably insist that I address him as Oscar the Gigolo.

The squat, muscular man returned and placed silverware rolled up in a white paper napkin in front of me. "*Gracias*," I said. He placed another set in front of the plastic chair next to mine. I slid it across the table. He grinned and returned to a stool beside the door, as though his job were to guard it. *From what? Aggressive tourists who shoved through the kitchen and garbage area?* To block the entrance, all he had to do was stand.

Could the secret dining room be an illegal business, or was I—a non-Cuban—eating there, the problem? The guard had already been stationed at the door when we arrived, so it didn't seem like I was the problem. Of course, if Oscar were a gigolo, they might expect him to bring illegal non-Cubans here on a regular basis.

Oscar returned with our drinks and took his seat across the table, not seeming surprised that his place setting was there. Maybe I had conveyed my lack of interest. He sipped from a sweating can of beer. I sipped from my tepid bottle of water. An uncomfortable silence settled until someone kicked at the door.

The guard opened it and the dishwasher delivered two steaming plates to our table. The boy stood there a moment before Oscar shooed him away. Oscar and I unrolled our napkins, exchanged a look, and dove into our food. We ate with no talk for a solid two minutes. I realized that Oscar was as starved as I was, and just as relieved that this was not a "date." We didn't have to take civilized bites or worry if the skins of the black beans stuck in our teeth.

Finally he said, "How's the fish?"

"Fabulous." Honestly, the fish tasted fresh but whatever it was fried in seemed suspect. However, nothing is a better cook than an appetite.

Oscar pointed at the rice and beans. "And the *cristianos y moros*?"

"Excellent." I tried to imagine calling white rice and black beans Christians and Moors in the United States. I stirred my rice and beans together to give the rice some flavor. "You're a biologist, right?"

Oscar nodded and chewed.

I shoveled rice and beans into my mouth and whirled the prongs of my fork in the air until my mouth was empty enough for me to ask, "Do you know anything about scorpions and this supposed cancer cure?"

"It is not so ridiculous. The guy who discovered Escozul

was a biologist at Guantanamo. He tested the venom on cancer tumors in rats and dogs."

He pointed his fork at me. "About eighty-five percent of the rats survived. The proteins in the venom apparently inhibit the growth of tumors. At the same time, the immune system of the benign cells seems to increase."

I stared at him, unable to take another bite. He had told me he was a biologist, but I had not actually expected him to sound like one. "So Escozul may be a cure for cancer?"

He gave me a shoulders-to-ear shrug. "The biologist is not a doctor. Escozul has not been through clinical trials."

"What about people like the Duarte's daughter? She was cured, right?"

"She probably continued her other treatments. Most people do. So the answer to that question…." He let the thought trail off since there was no answer to the question of whether or not the venom had cured her.

Megan Melquist, however, had not continued her other treatments. Her life hung on the answer to that question. Anxiety bubbled up in me. Lucille's words bounced around in my head: *Let me know if she's alive.* What did she want me to do if I wasn't in time—if Megan was dead? I smashed beans on my plate, a satisfying stress reducer like popping bubbles on bubble wrap.

"If Escozul has promise, you'd think big pharmaceutical companies would be all over the drug." I wanted Oscar to be more definitive, hopefully to reassure me, to tell me this scorpion venom was what the world awaited.

"This is Cuba. Doing business here is problematic." He drained his beer. "Don't you like the beans?"

He sounded worried, so I forked up a big mouthful. When I had cleared my plate, Oscar paid the bouncer guy with the twenty CUC I had given him. The bouncer gave him change, but Oscar didn't volunteer to return it to me.

"Thanks for the meal," he said.

The guard had left, so Oscar held open the door into the garbage area. We scrambled across the stinky cubicle, through the kitchen, and past diners at the regular tables. When we reached the sidewalk and were walking side by side, I said, "That seems like a great deal—two dinners with drinks for under twenty bucks."

He gave me a small smile, but didn't reply. At the car, he ducked into the driver's side with no attempt to open my door for me. Maybe all he had wanted was a hot meal. He fired up the Yank Tank and the car thumped off the sidewalk.

With my tummy full, I relaxed. If Oscar with his cologne and tight clothing was a gigolo, I had established my lack of interest. My mind flitted to Briget and Ingrid, down in Cuba partly for the hot men. All the languages they spoke opened a lot of options.

I recognized my street when Oscar turned on to it. The bumpy cobblestones, towering buildings, and crisscrossed power lines were already familiar—my home away from home. Everything seemed less scary in the afternoon light. Oscar stayed behind the wheel when I got out. As I dragged myself up the three flights of cracked marble stairs to my *casa particular*, I thought about how additional languages enriched our lives. Thinking about languages reminded me of Megan's fluent French. I arrived at the fourth-floor Old Havana flat slightly out of breath. I turned the key, and with the snick of the deadbolt, the niggly exploded into my awareness.

I had made two blunders—evaluating the situation in Jagüey from an egocentric stance that assumed my quarry was like me, and dismissing a witness's value as a result. I remained on the dim landing outside the door to the *casa particular* taking plenty of time to beat myself up. My mom, who had not been outgoing and had disliked quite a few people, had nevertheless instructed me early and often never, ever, to throw away people. She would have made a better private investigator than I was. My mother would have been patient enough not to make the mistake I had.

The landing was dark except for light that rose up the stairwell and slid from under the *casa*'s door, but I remained in the darkness to compose myself, angry at my stupidity and sad at the sudden memory of my mom. Not a single thought about her had skimmed across my mind since I'd left California. She was slipping from my daily thoughts.

Oscar was long gone. But even if we returned to Jagüey, the French woman Colette would be gone, too, so I remained outside the door kicking myself. I saw it all: Megan and Colette meeting in line at the Duarte residence in Jagüey, two people who spoke French, and I imagined them gravitating toward each other like magnets, chatting to pass the long wait—maybe recommending favorite haunts to one another. I thought of all the French tumbling from Colette's mouth to her chauffeur, and the short version he'd relayed to Oscar. In my impatience to get down to specifics—like Megan's address—I'd let those French words float off into the air like chaff. I had not asked Oscar to pursue the stuff the chauffeur had deigned unimportant. Colette had not been able to supply an address, but if I'd had more patience, she might have narrowed greater Havana down to a neighborhood.

After a couple of minutes outside the door, I noticed the sound of the television and realized the viewers must have heard the slide of the deadbolt. They might be wondering why no one entered. I opened the door. In the living room, a woman was sitting up watching television, her dyed blond hair pressed back against a doily. On the maroon couch, a barefooted, teenaged girl rested with her head in the woman's lap. Their comfortable, proprietary manner suggested they were Alonso's wife and daughter. They barely glanced up to greet me.

I asked if I could use the phone. The woman nodded and I walked around the corner to the sideboard along the table. The phone sat beside the safe. I pulled Oscar's card from my pack, pushed the numbers, left a message, and hoped that he was now on his way home, rather than trolling Havana for fares—or women.

CHAPTER TWENTY

Eric didn't have a plan. He liked the saying, "Man plans and God laughs." Not that he believed in God, but plans were laughable. He preferred to move from moment to moment, and at this moment he stepped across the Duarte threshold.

The family conducted business at a round dining table, but the father and daughter both wore white lab coats to make the whole scam seem more official. The table had a computer monitor on it with cables dangling down that brushed Eric's knees when he sat. The father hovered, staring at him, but the girl seated herself.

She typed in the basic information. He was good at making up stuff. He'd already given her the name. They had no use for a social security number here. Address? He gave them the address of Aaron Phelps.

Type of cancer?

The first thing that popped into his mind was prostate

because one of his collectors had had it. But that guy had been fine. Apparently it was treatable. When cancer went for the nut sack, scientists got busy to find a cure.

"Liver," Eric said. The father and daughter exchanged a look that told him he had chosen well.

"Is your make-up to conceal jaundice?" the daughter asked tenderly.

"Yes." He was glad that she wasn't his type—too dark. He didn't want that kind of distraction right now.

"Do you have hepatitis?" she asked.

"Yes."

Her fingers flew over the keyboard. "Type?"

Eric knew hepatitis came in an alphabet soup, and more than one answer would be "correct" or there would be no question. "B," he said.

"Do you know how and when you contracted the hepatitis?"

"Why is it necessary to ask me these personal questions?" He hit the perfect note of indignation—not too strong—just a hint of offense. He cast his eyes up to the father for the man-to-man contact.

The father said something in Spanish.

"I'm not even sure I want to do this treatment," Eric whined. "I'd like to get a better sense of the set-up here. Since I've already *contracted* one serious disease, I'm sure you can understand."

The daughter sat up like she'd been reamed. The father asked her a question, and she answered hotly in Spanish.

With his hands in front of his white lab coat, the father made subtle pushing down gestures. He spoke softly, soothingly to his daughter, calling her Lucy. *An American name?*

"Would you like a quick tour of our operation?" Lucy asked.

"I would appreciate that," Eric said. "A tour would greatly reassure me."

The father walked into the living room and turned down a

hallway. Eric regarded Lucy.

"We are very hygienic." She folded her arms over her lab coat.

Eric let the silence sit.

Lucy stood and glanced toward the hallway. "My brother Emilio will show you the lab."

Eric didn't answer. Her ass was round and hefty, a good meaty grip for each hand.

The father returned with Emilio, a tall skinny kid grinning with importance. Eric assessed the family dynamics. Emilio didn't usually get the attention here—Lucy was the miracle cure, the newsmaker, the raison d'être for everything the family was doing. Eric smiled to himself. There. He did know some French. Rising and extending his hand, Eric adopted an affirming smile for Emilio, although with the gum distorting his mouth, would his smile work its magic? The kid gawked at him with widened eyes. Eric firmly shook Emilio's hand, and said, "First baseman?"

"How did you know that?" The kid dropped Eric's hand as if it burned, but his grin widened.

A person might call it a lucky guess, but Eric never would. He'd founded it on the country's obsession with baseball, and what Eric had observed as a somewhat shorter populace. Emilio was lanky, with long arms and legs—just what you'd want at first base. You never saw a short first baseman. "A first baseman," he said to Emilio, endowing the words with gravitas, as though he'd said *a president* "receives hurled scooped-up bunts, and long throws from down the third-base line, while stretching to keep his toe on the bag."

"*El Trecho*! That is what they call me!" Emilio said. "That means Stretch."

Sweet. Could he have scored any better?

Eric followed Emilio down a short hallway, past the family's bedrooms and out a door into a spacious, added-on room full of terrariums of every size. They lined the walls on the floor, covered a hodgepodge of tables, and sat on shelves rigged up over the tables. Eric sniffed the room. The wood shavings and urine smell of a pet store hung in the humidity.

Emilio grinned at him. "You get used to it."

Eric supposed that was true, but he'd never liked pet stores, or even the idea of having a pet. He peered into the sandy bottom of the nearest terrarium. "Just a few scorpions per container?"

"Oh, no. That one has a million babies in it, but they are about the size of the sand."

"How do you extract the venom?"

"Carefully." Emilio smiled.

He'd no doubt delivered that line a few times in his life. The boy indicated the far corner of the room—the one part not filled with terrariums. It was set up like a high school chemistry lab—cheap black countertops and a couple of stainless steel sinks wiped shiny clean. Above the sinks, vials hung from slotted racks.

Eric slid a tiny Pyrex beaker from a rack. The kid watched him do it, but didn't tell him to stop. Ten milliliters, Eric estimated.

"You cup the tube around the scorpion's stinger and then irritate the scorpion. When it tries to sting, the venom runs down the beaker."

"Ever been stung?"

Emilio rolled his eyes. "A few times."

"Well, obviously it didn't kill you."

"The first couple of times it made me sick."

"But now?" Eric replaced the beaker.

"Now I don't get stung."

Eric meandered to the next terrarium. Why did these kids speak English, when the father didn't. This container held two scorpions whose bodies, without counting the tail, were over an inch long. "How do you pick up one of these suckers?"

Emilio's eyes narrowed. "You sure are interested in the

scorpions."

"I'm like that with everything I get into," Eric said. "Baseball, for instance. I know all the statistics, collect the cards...."

"Me, too!"

"You have a card collection?" Eric tingled. He had thought the kid might. Now everything was falling into place. You just couldn't achieve this perfection, this thrill, with a plan.

Emilio glanced down the hallway.

With one finger, Eric pushed the terrarium lid a fraction of an inch.

Emilio finished sliding it aside as Eric had hoped he would. The kid moved his hand around the outside of the glass. "I'm showing the scorpions I'm here, so they don't get nervous." Emilio lowered both hands into the terrarium toward one of the mature-looking scorpions. "The key is that they can't sting backward, so some people—like my dad—grab them by the tail." Emilio placed a flat left hand in front of one scorpion, but it turned away. He put the left hand in front of it again, and using his right thumb and index finger boosted the scorpion onto his palm. "Now she's ready for a ride to the lab." Instead he let the scorpion scuttle off his palm back to its sand. He replaced the lid. "They're really not dangerous if you know how to handle them."

"Doesn't look too hard," Eric said.

"It's not—if you stay calm."

Calm was Eric's strong suit. It was time for a diversionary tactic. "Any chance I could see your baseball card collection?"

"It's just Cuban leagues."

"I know about the Cuban leagues."

"You do?"

"I do."

As soon as Emilio left the room, Eric opened the cabinet under the lab counter. There were boxes of latex gloves, more vials, an opened bag of dog food, and a Pyrex coffee pot without a lid. He quickly examined the room and spotted a mug perched on the ledge of a table beside a terrarium. That might work.

He sauntered across the room. He heard a squeaky hinge. *The boy opening a closet door?* It didn't sound like the lab door, although the boy had left it ajar and it was gradually sagging more and more open. Eric picked up the mug, which was half-filled with black coffee. Taking it to a lab sink, he rinsed it, and then stooped down to grab a latex glove from the box. It could be stretched over the top of the mug to make a lid—just poke a few air holes.

"*¿Qué hace*?"

Eric looked toward the door. He didn't understand the father's words, but he could guess that the man was asking him what he was doing. The man must move like the air. Eric had not heard any footsteps.

A heavy ceramic mug dangled in his hand. If he whacked the man on the head, could he knock him out?

CHAPTER TWENTY-ONE

I felt restless waiting for Oscar to return my call. Even if my room had not been filled with a mattress on the floor, it was too small for satisfactory pacing. Staying in a *casa particular* entitled me to use the common areas of the house, but I already felt like an intruder.

I flopped on the mattress and recorded my expenses on a legal pad, writing dollars instead of CUC. Thinking about passing through customs on the return trip, I decided to refer to Havana as San Francisco and Jagüey as San Jose. I kept everything generic: lodging, meals, and transportation. My recordkeeping occupied all of five minutes.

Shifting to my right elbow, I reread the file on Megan Elizabeth Melquist. Her mother had almost died from preeclampsia, and a C-section had delivered Megan at thirty weeks—a very premature baby, which no doubt had amped up the intent focus on her as an only child. Why had

Lucille Barnhart included this detail? Was it a way to emphasize Megan's preciousness?

I scratched at my ankle and hoped the *casa* didn't have bed bugs. This case was irritating enough. I wasn't sure what Lucille wanted. She'd asked simply to know if her daughter was alive, but the request felt loaded with expectation. Of what, I didn't know. It was as if Lucille expected me to read her mind. She was too lofty to convey her desires. I was supposed to intuit them. To hell with that. I wasn't her maid in waiting. She'd hired me for one task.

I kicked myself again for not remembering Megan's fluency in French. She and Colette might not have shared addresses or phone numbers, but they could have chatted about good restaurants, favorite places for manicures, best local coffee houses—places that might have narrowed my search.

Unless I chanced upon Colette on a return visit to the Duarte house, I couldn't think of any way to chase down this lead except through Oscar. I hadn't seen any other chauffeured cars in Cuba. I hoped that Oscar might know how to contact Colette's driver. They had seemed to recognize each other.

I stood, stretched, tramped over my mattress, stepped up into the bathroom, turned around, hopped down, and bounced across the mattress to the other wall. I opened the window and looked down the airshaft, gray concrete all the way to the bare slab at the bottom. Cool damp air scented with propane wafted up the opening.

Waiting in this cell-like room would drive me crazy. As time passed, it became increasingly clear that if Oscar had headed home, answering my call was not at the top of his to-do list.

I pulled out my *Lonely Planet* and my map of Havana. Using the two, I plotted my route, seven blocks up to Obispo and then several blocks over to Mercaderes Street. Confident that I could make my way to Hotel Ambos Mundos without consulting the map or the book again, I sniffed the outfit I'd worn on the plane and deemed it acceptable. I changed into the more stylish clothing.

Across the dim hallway of Casa Maria the door to the other rental room stood ajar. Now, I wasn't an investigator for nothing. When I was a kid, I was so curious—or snoopy, as my brother Donald called it—that my mom nicknamed me "Carol Cat." But honestly, how could anyone not want to see the other room offered by the *casa particular*? Maybe it had a better bed, and I would want to move there for the night even if the bathroom didn't adjoin it.

I stepped across the hall and peeked in. Fully dressed in her black skirt and blouse, Maria lay completely still on her back. Her eyes were shut. She'd parked her black shoes, molded to the shape of her feet, side by side at the foot of the bed. She stretched, unmoving, atop the flowered bedspread. Why was she sleeping in the guest room? Was she sleeping? I stuck my head fully through the door. To my relief, she emitted a soft snore.

I backed away. It struck me that given the dimensions of the flat, the family's private quarters off the side hallway couldn't amount to much—possibly one room—and that the family members might sleep where and when they could. No wonder the mother and daughter sprawled in front of the television when I had entered. The situation made me uncomfortable enough to want to check out of the *casa* at the same time I recognized their dire need for my money.

After filling my water bottle from the large bottles in the refrigerator, I passed the long dining table and entered the living room. The mother and daughter ignored me at first, but then the mother glanced up from the *telenovela*. I hated to interrupt their soap opera.

An ornate wall clock, a sixties relic with gold-colored shooting spires of metal all around it, decorated the wall. I announced in Spanish that I would return at seven o'clock, and that if Oscar called, to please ask him to call me then, that it was important.

The mother replied that my message was clear. I was

unconvinced. She returned her dull gaze to the television. The daughter didn't even lift her head. They had, I guessed, become inured to people streaming through their home. They couldn't invest emotional energy in me. They had to concentrate on how to sleep sitting up or sprawled on the couch. At the last moment, some deep intuitive part of me that has saved my bacon more than once, added, "Please tell him that I've walked to Hotel Ambos Mundos."

Locking the regular lock and the deadbolt, I maneuvered my way down the cracked marble steps. Clearly any money the families made went into their individual flats, and not into the common areas. I pushed my way out the battered colonial door into dwindling sunlight. As I turned the corner and headed toward Obispo, a bike cart rang its bell and zipped around a group of small girls in formal yellow dresses and ribbons practicing a dance in the middle of the cobblestones.

I stepped off the narrow sidewalk to let an elderly man on crutches get by. His white shirt was frayed around the collar and his brown polyester pants were slick with age, but the bandage on his foot appeared professionally wrapped and his aluminum crutches fit him.

For several blocks, I picked my way through the neighborhood, the streets shadowed by the tall buildings. In the fading light, the residents hauled in laundry from overhead lines, chatted across the street from window to window, and played dominoes outside doorways. As I neared Obispo Street, a man stepped out of a shop. He played a rhythm on an instrument like a woodblock, trying to entice me into the store. Another man popped up the lid of a box of cigars and made his pitch to me, but unlike in Santa Cruz, no one begged for money. No one occupied an entranceway staked out with crushed cardboard. No one passed with the stench of his sleeping bag bobbing by my nose. I didn't have to keep an eye on the sidewalk for dog feces or worse.

There must be a police presence, but I didn't see any.

The pink Hotel Ambos Mundos stood on the sidewalk. It wasn't an imposing building—five floors, maybe ten rooms per floor.

My eyes rose up the blocky façade broken by small balconies. Above the entrance fluttered a Cuban flag and a flag that I guessed must be for the Havana Province. The lobby's tile was in perfect condition, and the couches looked so soft and clean that I wanted to plop down and take a nap. What was I doing staying in Casa Maria for another night?

In back of the couches, a pianist played soft jazz on a grand piano near large windows with views to the streets. The rattan stools along the glossy, dark bar begged me to sit down and sip a mojito. I passed it all by. Registration was at the back of the lobby along with a row of desks for tourist information and tour arrangements.

"I'm here to meet Mr. Aaron Phelps," I said. "Has he registered?"

The woman at the registration counter wore a scarf about her neck and expertly applied make-up. "We do not have any Aaron Phelps." She offered to take my name, and to let him contact me should he become a guest of the hotel.

"He's probably just not here yet. I'll wait."

Black and white photographs of Hemingway covered the walls, and I moved close to read the captions. Hemingway had been a regular guest in room 511 of Hotel Ambos Mundos and the room was preserved like a mini-museum with regular tours. I remembered what Brittany had told me about her and Megan being the kids in class who read the books. They had both gone on to major in lit.

I asked one of the uniformed tour agent women for the time. If I went right now, I could catch the last tour of the day. It might be better not to ambush the strange man Aaron Phelps as he entered the hotel, anyway. He might be more amenable to helping me if I let him check in and get comfortable, although truthfully, I didn't know how he could aid my search for

Megan, unless, miraculously, she had decided to contact him this very day. I was snatching at air, but maybe I'd missed something with Aaron Phelps, the way I had with Colette Delvaux.

Following the doorman's directions, I rode an old-timey cage elevator to the fifth floor. The hallway was deserted, but a large metal relief of Hemingway's visage made the corner room easy to spot. In Spanish, a plaque proclaimed that the novelist, ERNEST HEMINGWAY, lived in this room during the 1930's.

No one was around, so I tried the door. It was locked. Since a tour was scheduled, I knocked. A young woman answered with her purse in hand.

"I'm here for the tour."

She smiled tiredly.

"Do you speak English?" I asked.

"Of course."

"You don't have to show me around." The room was tiny. In the center Hemingway's glass-encased typewriter sat on a desk. The writer had a view out opened accordion doors over the rooftops of Havana fading now into the tropical night. The placard outside the room must have meant Hemingway "stayed" not "lived" here. I couldn't imagine the burly man in the downstairs photographs "living" in these cramped quarters. The cordoned-off double bed in the corner looked so small that he would have had to sleep at a diagonal. I wondered if he was married then. I tried to imagine two people pushed together in the bed in a room with no air conditioner on a sultry Havana night. With his chest hair, Hemingway looked like the kind of man who would sweat.

I prowled the room as the docent watched me. The room didn't need a docent so much as a guard. A glass-fronted bookcase exhibited inscribed Spanish-language editions of Hemingway's books. Atop the case sat a model of his boat—The Pilar.

I crossed the room to a door near the entrance.

"Oh, that is just the bathroom," the guide said.

"Is it okay to look at it?"

"It is okay."

The bathroom held the basics with enough room to turn around. No, I concluded, the Hemingway of legend did not "live" in this confining space. It was a place to write and to flop. The rest of the time he would have been out carousing in Havana's bars or fishing on his boat. The Hemingway of legend was not a person to be caged up in a small room like this. Nor was I. I backed out of the bathroom.

"Do many Americans take this tour?"

"Not so many."

"In the last couple of months have you seen…"

The tour guide wagged her head in anticipation of an impossible query.

"…a very tall, slender American woman…"

She continued to shake her head.

"…early thirties…"

She added a tired sigh to the head wagging.

"…no hair…"

She stopped shaking her head and nodded. "Yes. I've seen her."

I froze. "You have?"

"Yes. She came here." She scratched at the top of her neck. "Maybe a month ago. She asked many acute questions."

I was standing right in Megan's tracks—too bad the trail was cold.

Time for another check on Aaron.

CHAPTER TWENTY-TWO

Eric Mars stared at Mr. Duarte. He didn't like the man. He didn't like anyone who got in his way. But if he killed him with the coffee mug, he'd have to dispose of the body, and the son would be returning to the lab at any second. There was nothing to be gained beyond personal enjoyment by bashing in the guy's skull. The idea of telling the man he was getting a drink flitted through his mind, but no tourist would take water from the tap.

Instead he said in Aaron Phelps' stilted English, "Pardon me. I have OCD. I saw the dirty coffee cup, and," he twirled his hand in the air, "felt compelled to wash it."

Mr. Duarte furrowed his forehead, looking from Eric's face to the mug and back, pausing on the latex glove.

Eric Mars hoisted the latex glove and with a smile said, "Part of my OCD." He didn't think the man understood any of it except his tone. Maybe the "pardon me," because Eric had heard something like *pardona* me on the street. The main thing was to be reassuring—not to appear guilty, or nervous, or evasive.

"Emilio!" Mr. Duarte barked.

The young man, toting a battered shoebox, appeared behind Mr. Duarte.

The father launched into rapid Spanish accompanied by gesticulating at the lab, at the mug, at Eric Mars. Finally Emilio responded, and Eric could tell that he was hurt and angry, resentful. Everything in the house revolved around his sister, cancer, the miracle cure, the scorpions.... Nobody cared about Emilio's dreams tucked away in a gray cardboard box.

Couldn't be better, Eric thought.

When the heated exchange reached a lull, Eric offered his Obsessive Compulsive Disorder explanation to Emilio.

Emilio waved off the explanation like it was unimportant. He sat the ripped shoebox on the counter by the sink. The father delivered another angry tirade, spun on his heels, and retreated down the hallway.

Eric didn't have any scorpions yet, but other than that, things were going swimmingly. He needed to play out the scene, be patient, not get physical. Emilio was thin, but taller than he was, and young and athletic. Right now the kid trusted him, or at least was so eager to talk baseball that he disregarded his father's anger and the strangeness of Aaron Phelps.

Emilio wiggled off the box top and placed it on a terrarium lid. All four corners of the box were starting to split, but inside the cards ran in two neat rows with rectangles of plain paper between each card, separating them, protecting them, labeling them.

"Would you happen to have a Minnie Miñoso?" Eric heard the excitement in his own voice. He could jerk off to a perfect Minnie Miñoso. He had a client ready to pay top dollar for the card.

Emilio beamed. "Minnie Miñoso? You know Minnie Miñoso?"

"Sure. Saturnino Orestes Arma Minnie Miñoso Arrieta. The Cuban Comet. I told you I'm a Cuban league fan."

Emilio didn't have to riffle through the cards. "I have two Minnie Miñosos." He plucked out the first card, with a bent corner. He extracted the second—perfect edges, well centered and rare, a black and white from Miñoso's days in the sugar mill league. Eric thought he might cum in his pants—no work necessary.

Now to find out how much the card was worth to this avid, but amateur and relatively poor, collector. Not as much as the value to an American collector filling a void.

"I am thirty-five years old, and I must have that Minnie Miñoso." Instead of his wad of CUC, Eric pulled out a crisp American one-hundred-dollar bill that he always carried with him.

But the kid's eyes didn't latch on to the money. He stared at Eric's stomach. "Why do you have a pillow in your pants?"

"Oh, that," Eric chuckled. "That helps with the pain from the liver cancer." He held an edge of the bill with each hand and popped it together and open a few times to focus Emilio's attention.

"One hundred and fifty."

"One hundred twenty-five and you give me a couple of those scorpions."

As Eric rode the air-conditioned bus for tourists back to Havana, he cradled the ceramic mug in his lap. He'd seen the woman across the aisle peeking at the perforated latex glove stretched over the top.

He smiled at her. She was blonde, but too old and too skinny. "Scorpions," he said.

She didn't seem frightened or put off.

"Scorpions," he repeated, thinking the woman might not have heard him.

Her complacency remained intact. She must not speak

English.

Then she said, "Fascinating creatures."

Another damn Canadian.

"Isn't the air-conditioning cold for them?" she asked.

Eric turned forward. His skin bubbled with anger like simmering water. He placed the mug between his thighs and tugged the tail of the guayabera over it. They had better fucking survive. The scorpions were perfect, so intimate. If Megan wanted scorpion venom, he'd give her scorpion venom. The poetic justice was exquisite.

The Canadian woman shot him a glance and turned to the man in the window seat of her row. She bent her head toward the man and whispered.

The bitch. It was a good thing he had not procured a knife. He would plunge it through her scrawny chest.

Except for this stupid woman, he was pleased with the way events had turned out. That showed the wisdom of following where life led, of living in the moment. He was a Zen type of guy.

He moved to an empty seat near the back, where the Canadian woman and the man would have to rear up over the high seats and twist to see him. He settled into the plush fabric. The scorpions scuttled against the ceramic. He checked to make sure the latex glove was secure over the top and then repositioned the mug between his legs. He dug out the wads of gum behind his lips and stuck them under the armrest.

The Canadian woman's words had stirred up some anxiety. Emilio had scooped sand into the bottom of the mug and thrown in a few kibbles of dog food, which he claimed the scorpions would eat. Eric didn't know how long the kibbles would last, though. He needed to find Megan. He smiled at the thought of the American private detective, tracking down Megan for him while he relaxed in the comfortable bus. Again life had delivered. The next morning he would be at her *casa particular* ready to follow her.

The green flat land rolled by outside his window. He tilted the seat back and thought of Megan stretched naked on his hotel bed, even though he'd be in a different hotel that night. The drapes would be open and her flawless creamy skin would shimmer in the moonlight. Her hands would be tied to the headboard with his shoelaces, and she would lie like she used to, her eyes full of longing and love, waiting for the gift he had promised her.

He would run his hands softly up and down her inner thighs as she liked. He'd whisper in her ear exactly what he intended to do, but it wouldn't matter. The puffs of air, his tongue at the top of her lobe, would drive her crazy with desire.

Then he would dump the first scorpion on her smooth belly.

CHAPTER TWENTY-THREE

Megan rode in a state-sanctioned taxi back toward central Havana. Her baptism by the babalao had elicited her favorite feeling. If she were a religious person, she might call it ecstatic, but she wasn't, so she settled for thrilled.

The thrill was almost as good as her times with Eric. She had met him at the Red Room. All he did was stand and hold out his hand, and she had been hooked. Without even touching her, he reeled her toward him. When their fingers met, the jolt made her sink, light-headed, into the booth. She thought of God's hand reaching toward Adam's on the Sistine Chapel ceiling. When their two hands connected, this is how it would feel.

For all that, their relationship had started normally enough with margaritas at the bar. Later there were kisses up her legs, soft as butterfly flutters, whispers of her erotic beauty up her neck, her back arching with desire. It had slowly evolved into cocaine and spanks and slaps, the best sex of her life, until one day she found herself with her hair yanked back and the tip of a knife dipping into her neck.

She had moaned with pleasure even then, but as soon as she was away from Eric, she had started to shake. When she was safe in her apartment, she had inspected the nick on her neck and knew next time it would be longer. She was on a ride with only one possible outcome for her.

The cabbie lit up a cigarette. He sucked until his cheeks hollowed and exhaled a long jet. Megan inhaled the smoke deep into her lungs. She loved the smell of pipes and cigarettes and doobies while they were burning. Everything about smoking appealed to her—the red embers and consummation. But afterward—that was the problem. Nothing stank worse than the clothing and breath of a smoker. Nothing was more bitter and cold than ash.

A flush of nausea rose up from her stomach, heated her cheeks, and made her eyes water. She opened the window of the taxi, and cool air rushed in. She tried to get back to the thrill of the ceremony, the babalao pronouncing, "You are now part of Palo Monte, daughter of Tierra Tiembla, known as Obatala." His declaration had washed over her, filling her with power. Did it even matter whether the power of the orishas was real or not? Perhaps it was enough to have a ceremony where someone declared you powerful. Eric's obsession with her had provided the same taste of omnipotence.

Megan remembered her friend Brittany asking, "If it's excitement you want, why not just ride rollercoasters?" Megan smiled at the memory, in part because she had. She'd ridden roller coasters from the wooden one at the Santa Cruz Beach Boardwalk to the incredible Steel Dragon 2000 in Mei, Japan. She'd outgrown rollercoasters before she had even met Brittany and graduated to mountain climbing.

She missed her friend—missed the whole sprawling Bañuelos family. She had been rocked in the comfort of their noise and size—big enough to embrace any dysfunction. If half of the family was mad at you, that still left plenty of people to talk to.

In the Bañuelos' house, with its banging screen door and aroma of enchiladas, she could rest, like in a boat rocking on a gentle sea. At the Bañuelos', she was surrounded by people who liked her, but whose energy and attention fractured in a thousand directions. Would she feel like a normal person if she'd grown up in that household instead of with Lucille? She shuddered. She knew her mother loved her in her own way. Megan had known since she was five years old that she had been a miracle baby. She knew every detail of Lucille's difficult pregnancy, the months confined to bed, the premature birth, but at home with Lucille, every movement felt sharp and brittle.

After she'd screamed at her father and he'd fallen down dead in the driveway, Megan understood that Lucille had been right to send her to counseling. But her mother and the psychologist could say "brain aneurysm" all they wanted, Megan knew she had killed her dad. She had caused the vessel to pop. She held on to both the guilt and the power of it.

The sessions wore on for weeks until she opted to pair the words "Lucille" and "emotional abuse." The result was instantaneous. The same day, her mother decided she didn't need therapy any more.

Megan shook away thoughts of her mother. Their relationship was beyond repair. She watched tin-roofed shacks pass by, interrupted periodically by many-storied tenements. The high rises looked like the failed housing projects from the sixties in the United States. Supposedly Castro had helped the poor. What had their conditions been like before the revolution?

The taxi driver crushed the butt of his cigarette into the ashtray. He was solemn and silent, but she caught him looking in the rearview, casting curious glances at her—a pale Americana in the white dress of a Santeria initiate, not an everyday sight. She smiled at him, then demurely looked down, and knew he would see her as so many did—delicate and quiet, mysterious perhaps—like a pale stingray gliding under water.

It would be a lethal mistake to step on one.

CHAPTER TWENTY-FOUR

The woman at the counter shook her head before I even asked. "Aaron Phelps is still not registered."

I took a stool at the bar and ordered a mojito. From the hotel, light spilled out onto the sidewalk. With my back to the counter, I could watch the main entrance, the side entrance by the piano, the elevator cage, and the bottom of the staircase. When the icy drink arrived, I gave the waiter a five CUC bill.

"Keep the change." I might have to occupy the seat for a while and hoped to establish good will without getting drunk on my butt.

I nursed the drink—the tangy lime offset by the sweetness of the rum and added sugar—too much sugar. The piano player's long fingers danced over the ivories, playing a song I didn't know. It had a syncopated beat and romantic melody that struck me as authentically Cuban. When the pianist glanced up at me, I applauded.

Other than the bartender, I was the only person in the bar, but people on the sidewalk also clapped. The piano player, encouraged by the attention, departed from the melody, running his fingers from one end of the keyboard to the other in what appeared to be an improvised jam. I was so caught up in the performance that I almost missed Oscar when he appeared at the main entrance.

Aaron Phelps would have to wait. The French woman lead seemed more promising. Oscar drove me back to my *casa particular* and followed me up the dark staircase.

"This marble is from Cuba."

"Really?" Under the dirt, the beauty of the pale gray stone remained, but I didn't know how he could even see it now.

"Pay attention. You will see marble everywhere in Cuba. Cuba is famous for marble."

By the fourth floor, both of us were breathing too hard to want to chitchat. When I opened the door to the flat, the mother, rubbing her eyes, pulled herself up from the couch. When she saw Oscar, her eyebrows shot up in alarm. She greeted him politely in Spanish, and then looked at me.

"He's my driver."

She gestured for me to follow her and we turned the corner into the dining area. "We do not allow overnight guests," she whispered in Spanish.

I blinked. *Me and Oscar on the lumpy mattress on the floor?* Even though I had speculated Oscar could be a gigolo, the woman's words rendered me speechless—for two seconds.

"I brought Oscar here to make some phone calls for me," I said in Spanish. "May we use the telephone?"

She planted fists on her hips, as though my request was a ruse to get Oscar past the living room so I could sprint down the hall and lock him into my bedroom.

After a moment, she stuck her hand around the wall and motioned for Oscar to come. She stood sentinel as Oscar called a family, a family he'd known since grade school, the chauffeur's family. From there he called the chauffeur.

This ended up being a long conversation, of which I heard one side, and that in rapid Cuban Spanish. The gist, though, was that the chauffeur, Jose, did not want to risk his job. Each time Oscar's argument flagged, I raised an additional finger to add another hundred CUC to the pot. It was, after all, Lucille's money, and the people down here needed it. Castro would have been proud of my redistribution of wealth. At five fingers, a deal was struck, and we had an address. But not a French translator. I guess it was a matter of plausible deniability. As long as the chauffeur didn't show up at Colette's, someone might believe he didn't know how we had found her.

After the phone call, Oscar and I stood in the dining room, squeezed between the table and the sideboard.

Oscar pursed his lips and scratched a thick eyebrow. He cocked his head. "What do you want to do?"

"I know some other people in Cuba who speak French."

"Okay."

"They're in Viñales."

"That is two and a half hours away."

"I have a cell number."

I retreated to my room, dug around in my pack, and returned with Briget's cell number. When I punched in the numbers, nothing happened—no ring, no busy signal, no squawk. I hung up the phone. "I remember the name of their *casa*. Home Sweet Home."

The family kept a phone book on the sideboard. I paged through it, found the number, and went into the living room to ask Alonso's wife for permission to call Viñales.

"If it is short," she said in Spanish. Otherwise they would have to charge.

I nodded. I didn't expect the call to be short, but it was. The owner of the establishment answered the phone. Ingrid and Briget had gone out. No, she didn't know when they would return.

Oscar leaned against the sideboard. On the opposite wall hung framed photos of the family along with one of Fidel Castro. Oscar wrinkled his forehead. "What do we do?"

He had really slipped into this *we* business. I twisted around my lips, which helped me think. Maybe it pulled my scalp around in a way that woke up my brain. If we drove across town now, we would arrive at Colette's in the dark at an hour when an unexpected knock on the door might be startling, and we would have no way to communicate with her. Tomorrow I might not have a solution to the latter problem, but at least I wouldn't frighten the woman. As much as I hated to wait, I was exhausted and in no condition to patch together a narrative from bits of English, Spanish and French.

"*Mañana*," I said.

CHAPTER TWENTY-FIVE

At the Havana bus station, Eric scrubbed the make-up from his face. He stuffed the pillow into a garbage can, sauntered to the curb and caught a cab to his hotel to pick up his stored luggage. In the lobby restroom he shaved off the black soul patch and changed into a Hawaiian shirt.

Back on the street, Eric selected a new cab and ordered the driver on to Hotel Ambos Mundos. The cabbie took a route along the dark Malecón. Water splashed and sprayed over the seawall. Eric supposed some people might find the black, moonlit water romantic. He thought it was spooky as hell.

The scorpions remained tranquil in the mug between his legs. Maybe they slept at night. Eric shook the cup and heard them scuttle. He slipped a tiny travel flashlight from a side pocket of his bag, peeled back the latex glove, and jiggled the cup as he shone the light into it. Both scorpions hoisted their stingers. That was good. It didn't take much to get them stirred up.

The cabbie drove up to the side of the hotel. He wagged his finger at Obispo Street. "No automobiles," he said by way of explanation.

"No worries." Eric passed forward the fare. He hopped out of the back seat, extended the handle of his bag, and let the wheels bang to the ground. Strolling through the entrance of the blocky building, he pulled his suitcase with one hand and held the coffee cup in the other. He strode directly back to the reception desk and registered as Eric Mars, requesting a top-floor room.

The woman at the counter wore red lipstick, a uniform and neck scarf, trying to look official. He guessed her to be of legal age, at least in the U.S., but she might not be old enough to drink—of course, that was U.S. law, too.

She perused the passport photo where he still had his thick hair and then eyed his bald head. Her smile was more than business polite. Even bald, he was a fine specimen, and if she didn't dig the cue-ball look, she'd just glimpsed how he would appear when he grew out his hair.

"We hope you enjoy your stay, Mr. Mars."

"I'm sure I will. I wonder if you would be so kind as to note some information on my registration."

"Certainly."

"I'm an author."

Her dark eyes lit up and carefully regarded him.

"Many readers know me better by my pen name. Even some of my friends call me by that name."

"Of course," she said. "Would you like me to note your pseudonym?"

"Yes." Her impeccable English impressed Eric, but hey, if they had a university down here for clowns, they probably had one to train hospitality workers.

"And that name is?"

"Aaron Phelps."

"Really?" She cocked an eyebrow.

Eric's stomach lurched. Other than her inviting smile, the woman had not given the slightest hint of anything but professionalism, so the question set off an alarm.

"Really," he stated. "Why do you ask?"

She flushed. "I do apologize."

"I'm not offended," Eric said. "I just want to know why you asked."

She bit her lip, scraping away some of the perfect application of red. "I like the name Eric Mars better."

"Me too, Gorgeous." He sat the mug down on the counter in order to pass her a ten CUC note.

The young woman peeped at the latex glove. Her blush receded and her face retracted into composure. "What do you have in there?"

"Deadly scorpions." He chuckled.

The receptionist giggled.

"Nah," he said. "That's an improvised lid for my coffee." He paused. "I know down here no one has heard of me," Eric said, "but I'm a hot item in the States. I even have a bona fide stalker—a woman."

"A stalker? Sorry, what is a stalker?"

This was annoying, but Eric hid his impatience. "Someone who follows you around. Like a hunter."

"Oh," she said, "*una acosadora*."

Whatever. Her eyes looked concerned, so that was probably right. "Please put through phone calls for Aaron Phelps, but if a woman shows up here in person, asking for Aaron Phelps, it's probably my stalker. Please alert me. Do not let her know my room number."

"Of course." The clerk lowered her lashes. "You are like Hemingway then?"

"Maybe not quite that famous."

"Women pursued him, too."

She raised her face. If she were blonde, she would be lovely.

"Legend holds that Jane Mason climbed along the fifth-story ledge of our hotel to gain access to Hemingway's room."

"Is that so?" He smiled. "I'll keep my window closed."

She smiled.

"What time did you start your shift?" he asked.

"I just started. I cover the night shift." She waited.

"Will you please pass this information on to the morning workers?"

"Yes. Of course. Is there anything else I should do if this woman arrives? Is she dangerous?"

"Nah." Eric shook his head. "She's completely harmless." He gave the baby-doll receptionist his practiced smile and met her eyes, a second longer than necessary. He wanted to keep alive whatever fantasy she might be nursing.

He picked up the mug and ambled to the lobby, pulling his suitcase. He congratulated himself for his maneuver. The investigator—Carol What's'er Face—could show up here. He'd given her the name of this hotel. She had those photos and knew how he looked as Eric Mars, so that was a complication, but he'd taken care of it brilliantly. She would ask for Aaron Phelps, and he would be forewarned. Not that she posed a serious threat. Her mission was to find Megan, not him. But he didn't want the investigator screwing things up. To use her, he needed to stay ahead of her.

All was fine, he told himself. If the detective came to this hotel, it might save him the hassle of following her from her *casa particular*.

The lurch of the cage elevator interrupted his thoughts. Eric pulled open the grillwork door and admonished himself to be in the moment, because if you weren't *now here*, you were *nowhere*.

CHAPTER TWENTY-SIX

Megan didn't want to be a snob, but Casa Tranquilidad was wretched. The illegal *casa* had one room to rent and the bathroom was shared with family members, including two teenagers.

At the moment, the living room was blessedly empty, and she slipped through it to the good-sized side bedroom. She'd left open the window facing the quiet backyard. Now that she was alone, the babalao's words gripped her. *Death is looking for you.* The words helped to dispel the ambivalence she had felt since Lucy had reported Eric's appearance at the clinic. As a safeguard, Megan had shown the family Eric's photo, but she had not really believed he'd follow her all the way to Cuba.

She crossed the room, closed the window, and glanced around for something stick-like to wedge over the bottom pane. The room held a bed, lamp, and rickety dresser.

A framed painting of a landscape hung on the wall. Megan

took it down. Behind it the wallpaper stripes were yellow and the roses pink rather than brownish.

She turned the painting sideways and propped it on top of the bottom window frame. It didn't fill the gap, but if someone tried to lift the window from the outside, the painting would either topple on the floor, alerting her, or provide only a three-inch opening.

Eric had already shown up at the clinic once. Eventually he would find her. She was the obsession of the smartest, most gorgeous, craziest man she'd ever met. It had never seemed real. *Why her?* She wasn't beautiful or talented or sparkly.

She flopped down on the squishy mattress and splayed out in starfish position. She imagined herself back home, lying on the beach at the edge of the tide. The boost she'd gained from her visit to the orisha sucked out like sand under her body. She closed her eyes. Really, what did it matter if Eric found her? Overwhelming exhaustion flowed in to replace the dissipating energy.

Radiation, chemo, scorpion venom, a voodoo priest—nothing was working. Her body buoyed, as though floated into the water. When the pain became too much, Hemingway had gone out with a bang. But then, he'd given the world something to remember him by. What had she ever done except live up to her mother's worst expectations—that she'd amount to nothing.

She could not die another pathetic female victim. She simply could not.

The bang of the front door woke Megan. One of the family's teenagers yelled at the other. The mom scolded them. The door banged again.

Megan struggled to sit up, and blinked, disoriented that sunshine streamed through the window. *Had she really slept through the night?* Her scarf had come loose. She pulled it from her head and discarded it on the bed. She removed the necklace, but kept on the white clothing of a Santeria novitiate, ironing at the wrinkles with her hands.

Silence fell over the house. The father must have gone off to work, the kids to school. She pushed herself off the bed. The bathroom was all hers then.

After her toilette, Megan dragged herself to a round table covered with a waxy red-and-white checked cloth. The mother had told Megan that breakfast was included, and at the sound of the chair scraping, the matron peeked a weary, lined face from the kitchen. After a moment, she brought Megan a mug of instant coffee and thunked down a jar of milk with traces of powder along the rim. Her gaze lingered for a moment on Megan's blouse and skirt. Then she disappeared into the kitchen and returned. She slid a chipped plate in front of Megan on which rested two overripe bananas, cut lengthwise, and a sliced chunk of bread. Megan pulled off a piece and nibbled. It was stale.

The woman ducked into the kitchen as if to escape a complaint. Megan stood, holding on to the back of the chair. She tried to remember the word for egg. She had to eat something. "*¿Huevo?*"

The woman thrust her head out the doorway and held up one rigid finger. "*Uno.*"

"That's fine."

"*¿Revuelto? ¿Frito? ¿Hervido?*"

Megan surmised these were preparations for The Egg. The second one, *frito*, was almost the same word in French, but she didn't want fried, so she repeated the first word, which sounded like revolt. Given the quality of the other food, she hoped the word didn't mean revolting. She collapsed back into the chair. She had been feeling better, but that was before Eric had shown up and she had stopped going to the clinic.

The woman's flip-flops slapped back and forth across tile and the egg spat as it met grease. In a couple of minutes the woman placed in front of Megan a plate with a steaming scrambled egg on it. She smacked down a scrap of paper so hard

Megan's fork jumped. Printed in block letters were yesterday's date, the name Lucy Duarte, and her number.

"*Gracias.*" Megan's heartbeat accelerated. She could think of only one reason Lucy might call her. Eric. He had returned. The flowered skirt at the edge of Megan's vision became blurry. She crossed her arms on the table and lowered her head, pushing forward the plate.

"No eat?" the *casa* matron asked.

Megan slowly raised her head. "*Sí, sí.* Eat, eat."

The woman hovered and watched until Megan took a mouthful.

Megan reasoned that the word telephone sounded almost the same in French as in English, so it would probably be nearly the same in Spanish. After she swallowed the bite of egg, she ventured, "Telephone?"

With a knobby finger the woman tapped the number on the paper and launched into adamant Spanish. Megan didn't understand any of it except Mantanzas, the name of the province in which Jagüey was located, but she surmised the matron was upset about the cost of a long distance call. Megan pulled herself up.

"No eat?" The woman's voice raised another decibel.

Megan bobbed her head. "*Sí, sí.* Eat, eat. Moment-o."

Megan's mind floated behind her body as she crossed the living room to her quarters. She unzipped an inner hidden pocket of her bag, pulled out a handful of CUC, and returned to the table. The matron stood guard over the scrambled egg, her face set. Megan fanned out the bills and then pressed them into her hand. "Telephone?"

The woman stuffed the bills down the front of her grayish blouse. She didn't smile, but pointed to a black rotary phone in the living room. She must wonder, Megan thought, why an Americana with wads of money for expensive calls would be staying in a dump like this. The power of money sickened her.

The proprietor returned her hard stare at the egg. Megan

loaded a tiny bite atop the stale bread and forced herself to chew.

Lack of money had power, too, Megan thought. It dictated this woman's life from the need to take people into her home to her worry about wasting one egg.

After she had choked down the egg, Megan plopped into the chair beside the phone. The green fabric embraced her in squishy softness. She craved a real cup of coffee, but her favorite cafe was a mile away. Once a mile had been a nice walk. Now she didn't trust herself not to faint.

Lucy answered on the second ring.

"Thank God you have called." Lucy jumped into a story of a strange man who had visited with a shaved head and make-up on his face. "At first I thought they were because of his cancer, but he was so odd that I started to wonder if the whole thing could be a disguise."

Eric was a chameleon. Megan had seen him charm Lucille like a southern gent, and the same evening puff up like a gangster as he squared off with a bar bouncer. He had taken the pulse of her desires and made himself into the man of her dreams.

"I'm not sure it was him," Lucy continued. "Last time we only saw him for a moment, and this man looked completely different."

"What name did the guy use?"

"Aaron Phelps."

Megan swallowed a nervous giggle and closed her eyes. Aaron Phelps was a defense attorney with a bad hairpiece, a chubby collector of Mickey Mouse paraphernalia. She'd been to his house, where Aaron Phelps had knocked out bedroom walls to create a gallery for his unique passion. Aaron Phelps was also Eric's favorite drug dealer.

"Megan? Are you there?"

"Yes. Thanks to you and your family, Lucy, I am still here. And your suspicions are right," she added. "That was Eric."

Megan had to hand it to him. She had not fallen for just a cute face. Eric was clever. Determined.

"I am so sorry," Lucy said. "You warned us, but this man looked so different, I mean he was odd, but I did not even think of this possibility until later. I am so sorry."

"But you didn't tell him how to contact me."

"I did not tell anyone anything."

"What do you mean *anyone*?"

"A woman came here as well." Lucy paused. "A private investigator."

Megan drew a deep breath. Why was she surprised? Of course Lucille would use her money, exercise her power. From the moment Megan had been born—no, probably before that—from the moment she was conceived, Lucille had regarded her like a pet project. The woman had never been able to view her as a separate human being, entitled to her own life, including her own mistakes.

"What was the investigator's name?"

Lucy took a moment, as though she were checking, before she said, "Carol Sabala."

"What did she look like?" Megan asked, although she wasn't sure what difference it made.

"I don't know," Lucy sighed. "Even though her name is Sabala, she looked American. She was taller than I am. Maybe about five foot eight. She looked strong. Her hair was really short. Brown."

Megan closed her eyes and leaned her head back against the soft chair. "Were Eric and the detective there at the same time?"

"Yes."

Nausea roiled in her stomach. The presence of a private detective would accelerate Eric's actions. This development increased the urgency of what she had to do. "Do you know where Eric is staying?"

"No."

"Do you think anyone who came to the clinic that day

might know?"

"Possibly."

"Can you tell me who was there?"

The other end of the line was silent.

"This isn't a matter of confidentiality, Lucy." Megan heard traces of Eric's voice in her smooth, confident wielding. "Anybody driving by could have seen who was in the yard."

Megan listened to the hums and clicks in the phone line. "If I had been there yesterday," Megan said, "I would know."

Megan felt a presence and opened her eyes. The matron of the *casa* peeked her head into the room. The woman regarded her and the phone as if she thought she could extort another handful of cash.

"Does Eric speak Spanish or French?" Lucy asked.

"No." Megan sat up. *French*? That must mean that Colette had been in the line. Thank God Eric didn't speak French, although God only knew he might still have found a way to charm information from Colette. She glanced up. The proprietress remained peeking around the archway between the living room and dining room. Megan hardened her eyes, letting her gaze cut right through her. The woman retracted her head like a turtle. Megan snorted. She'd learned a thing or two from her time with Eric.

"Then your best bet to find out information about Eric would be the private investigator," Lucy said. "She wasn't our client. Do you have a pen and paper?"

Like she would really contact the investigator. Megan jotted down the number, anyway, thanked Lucy and hung up the phone. She tried to formulate a plan. Between the cancer and the treatments, thinking was labored and fuzzy, like a struggle through a cotton ball. It would help to know where Eric was right now. Maybe she could bargain with the detective and get her to reveal Eric's whereabouts—if she knew them. What could the P.I. actually do? She couldn't force Megan to return to the United States—unless Lucille ordered the woman to report her expired visitor's visa.

The proprietress reappeared and pointed at Megan. "You. *Huevo*. Tomorrow?"

Tomorrow must be a word like *mañana* that people knew even when they didn't speak the language.

"*Sí*." Megan said. It was the one breakfast item that had been edible. She craved a mug of strong Cuban coffee, something to revive her.

The woman heaved a sigh, collected a string bag by the front door, and left.

How could she have known that an egg meant a special shopping trip? She didn't chase after the woman to tell her to skip the egg. It felt pleasant to sit alone for a moment in the soft chair.

After a couple of minutes, she pushed herself up and wandered into the kitchen. She pulled open a drawer. It stuck at an angle and didn't contain anything but a jumble of silverware. She wiggled it shut and jerked out another. It clattered with a motley collection of kitchen tools. The family possessed two knives—a paring knife—too small to be much good, and a butcher knife with a nicked end. She ran its blade between her fingers. Someone kept the edge shiny and sharp. She set the precious item on the counter. If she took it, it would be missed.

Megan touched the small scar on her neck where Eric had pressed a knife. That should have been their last time together. She'd stopped calling and didn't return his messages, gauging that his response would be to flaunt a new girlfriend in her face by the end of the week.

At the memory of what did happen, Megan clutched the nicked butcher knife in front of her and swallowed down vomit. It had been rape, but she hadn't grasped that fully until she'd fled to Cuba. After all, people thought of him as her boyfriend. She'd been avoiding him, but she hadn't told him it was over. She had let him into the apartment. Her own mother would say she was "crazy about him." The best option had been to leave.

And here she was. She opened a cupboard in the *casa* kitchen. The plates and cups and pots didn't provide any useful weapon. She could hardly lug around a cast iron skillet. She glanced under the sink. She didn't recognize any of the brands of cleaning products. She squatted, opened a jar and sniffed. The strong vinegar zapped her sinuses like wasabi. She blinked. More cautiously, she unscrewed the cap from a jug that looked like bleach. It was. No doubt some of these products were poisonous, but how could she use them?

Bleach to the face would stop a person, even Eric. The thought made her stomach flip. Eric could have been a model, not for something lame like shirts or underwear, but for something sexy, like top shelf tequila. She wondered if bleach would disfigure his eyes.

Her heart hammered as she banged through the cupboards again, searching for a container with a top. Nothing.

She opened the refrigerator. The almost-bare metal racks didn't hold any containers that would work for carrying bleach. However, several ampules rattled in a side pocket. Packaged syringes rolled right beside them.

CHAPTER TWENTY-SEVEN

I'd promised Casa Maria that I'd spend another night. Now that I'd given Casa Maria as my contact place both to Aaron Phelps and to Lucy Duarte, I shouldn't switch hotels anyway. When I lay down, the mattress didn't seem quite as uncomfortable. That was my last thought.

The next morning, before I sat down to breakfast, I called Home Sweet Home in Viñales. The proprietor of the *casa* sounded bright and cheerful like she'd been up since dawn. Ingrid was another matter. She was groggy with sleep and slow to comprehend. However, when she grasped that I wanted her and Briget to return to Havana to help me with my investigation, she said, "Gumshoes?"

"Yes." I couldn't tell if she was excited about helping me or about her English, the way she had been excited when she invented the word *cellacracy*.

"Groovy."

I didn't have the heart to tell her Americans had stopped using the word thirty years ago.

As it turned out, the mountains in Viñales were beautiful, but the town was boring, and the two were planning to travel to Havana the next day. It didn't take much to convince her to move up her plans, wake Briget and catch the first bus to Havana. She even brushed aside my offer to cover their bus and taxi fares. I called Oscar and reserved him for the afternoon. He sounded happy to hear from me and eager to go.

I ate breakfast, showered, and gave my airplane outfit another sniff test. *Acceptable.* With a couple of hours left to kill before Ingrid and Briget's arrival, I filled my water bottle from the bottles in the 'fridge, threw my trusty pack over my shoulder, and headed down Obispo Street toward El Floridita bar. According to my guidebook, it had been a Hemingway hangout. If lit major Megan Melquist had toured Hemingway's room at Hotel Ambos Mundos, perhaps she'd visited Hemingway's bar as well. Maybe someone there could give me a lead.

The pedestrian street sparkled with morning freshness. At the first intersection, an ancient truck faced Obispo Street. Two men joked and laughed. One hefted bags of rice from Vietnam across the flatbed and down to the other worker who stacked them on the sidewalk.

A bicycle peddler rolled around the working men, pineapples and bananas bouncing in his cart. He shouted out his wares. A shopkeeper opened her door and gestured for me to come in. I smiled and continued, inhaling the hint of ocean air not yet masked by diesel.

My guidebook said that Havana had once been walled. Inside the gates lived the rich Spaniards and Cuban-born whites. One of the gates had been at Obispo and Monserrate, the location of El Floridita bar.

When I reached my destination, I didn't see any vestiges of the ancient gate. The bar was closed but inside workers stirred.

I peered through the windows at British Regency décor, wainscoting and wallpaper. A golden life-sized statue of Hemingway leaned in against the end of a long curved mahogany bar. This sure wasn't like J.J.'s former hangout back home. J.J.'s bar was open for breakfast, meaning it served coffee and could pop a burrito in the microwave.

I continued past the Museo Nacional de Bellas Artes and circumnavigated Parque Central, the beating heart of Havana. Cabs zipped around the square. Behind them, buses chugged, belching smoke. Yellow three-wheeled coco-taxis and bici-taxis whizzed along the outside of the traffic. Stately hotels edged the park, which had one of the ubiquitous statues of the poet José Marti at its center. I cut back toward El Floridita. This time I rapped on the window to get the attention of the workers. A red-coated bartender strode to the glass and pointed at a sign. The bar didn't open until 11:30. I mouthed that I just wanted to ask a few questions. He shook his head.

He strode back toward the bar, saying something to a guy scrubbing the floor, who glanced at me and then averted his eyes. The bartender disappeared through a door in the back. I cursed myself for not having money at the ready to plaster against the glass. On the other hand, I didn't want to pay for information every time if I didn't have to. It was Lucille's money, but wasteful spending cut against my grain.

At this intersection of Obispo and Monserrate, old American cars, waxed to high gloss, lined up waiting for fares. The drivers watched me expectantly, but I wanted to walk. Even though Ingrid and Briget could not possibly arrive for another hour, I hurried back to the *casa*, anxious not to miss them.

The home was deserted except for Maria, who stood in the kitchen pinching spice into a boiling pot of beans. I sniffed. Garlic and onion had been fried earlier, and right now Maria was adding cumin. "*Huele bien,*" I said. Smells good.

The old woman smiled. She wore the same black skirt and blouse that she had on the night I arrived and all day yesterday, but they remained tidy. I wondered if Alonso and his wife had seized the opportunity to sleep in the private area off the side hallway.

I went to my room, thought through the questions that I wanted to ask Colette, and waited for the girls. They arrived shortly before noon, both dressed in long shorts and baggy sweatshirts—so much for Euro fashion.

"New guests?" Maria asked in Spanish.

Brigit, Ingrid and I all exchanged glances. I stood behind Maria and tried to warn them with a subtle shake of the head, but it was apparently too subtle. "Sure. Why not?" Ingrid said.

Oscar arrived before Brigit and Ingrid had time to do more than register and throw their bags into their room.

As the three of us crossed the street to his taxi, Oscar grinned. He held open the back door for Ingrid and Briget and leered at Briget's bare, muscled legs as she slid across the bench seat. I climbed in the front.

"Look at that." Ingrid pointed at the dash. "An AM radio."

Oscar put his arm along the seat, twisted around, and beamed.

Briget leaned toward Ingrid, said something in French and they both giggled. Just a day and a half with Oscar and I already felt like he was my buddy. I didn't like the way they seemed to be enjoying a joke at his expense. I wanted to open the back door and pull the girls from the Chevy. However, I needed them for my investigation. Not to mention I didn't stand a chance toe-to-toe against either one of them.

As Oscar drove us eastward across Havana, the city changed. After Parque Central, the streets widened. At first the colonial buildings were crumbled with neglect like those in Old Havana. But the farther east we rode, the better preserved the old wealth of Havana became.

"This neighborhood is called Vedado." Oscar gestured at the leafy trees that ameliorated the buckled sidewalks. Lush yards concealed some of the need for paint. Water streaks down the facades, instead of seeming shabby, added to a sense of southern charm. We passed other palatial homes that shone with new white paint, their black wrought iron fences glossy.

"Some Cubans have money," I said.

Oscar cleared his throat. "A lot of these homes were confiscated and given to connected people in the party. There are always rumors about how rich Castro is." Oscar shrugged. "I don't believe them."

Brigit and Ingrid had seemingly inspired Oscar to new didactic tour-guide heights.

"Then there are the famous artists and athletes representing the glory of Cuba. They are treated well. They have cars and can travel outside the country.

"Other people have been making money in the new state-sanctioned businesses, or in the black market. And, of course, we have the people who live off their *gusano* relatives in Miami."

Oscar's remarks did not sound like someone enamored with the Communist party, but he still said *gusano* with contempt. *Gusano*, worm, was a term for a Cuban who had deserted the country with the fall of Batista. A person didn't have to love Castro to despise the former dictator and those who had grown fat and wealthy under his rule—the patriarchs of Cuban Miami.

Ingrid leaned over the seat. "So how do you feel about your government?"

Oscar lifted his shoulders to his ears and frowned at Ingrid.

She pressed forward until her face was a foot from his. Ingrid's jaw was too square and her eyes too small for her to be a beauty, but she was young and blonde, her smooth complexion rosy with health.

Oscar both puffed up and wiggled uncomfortably. "This is not a question for you to ask out there." The swing of his arm indicated all of Cuba. He stared forward, out over a falcon hood ornament, and turned the Chevy into a side street. "It doesn't matter what type of government you have. What matters is how they use their power."

"Do you think Castro uses his power in a good way?" I asked.

Oscar tugged at the neck of his tight shirt. "As a biologist, I appreciate that our president has set aside nature reserves and protected our coral reef."

"That would be popular in the town I'm from," I said to lighten the mood. "Santa Cruz is on a marine sanctuary."

"Your government is nothing to brag about."

The hotness in Oscar's statement indicated we had touched a nerve and one glib response from me wasn't about to calm his agitation.

"I'm no fan of George Bush," I said.

"Look at your country invading Afghanistan to capture a few terrorists." Oscar drove into a residential neighborhood. "Afghanistan did not attack the United States."

"But the terrorists are there."

"What did the people of Afghanistan do to deserve the destruction of their country?"

I decided that it was time for me to shut up and to let Ingrid torment Oscar. Instead Ingrid collapsed back into the seat and we traveled in silence. Oscar's comments resounded in my head. The images of the planes crashing into the World Trade Center were seared into our brains and most people in the United States weren't asking Oscar's question. Even peace loving Santa Cruz had turned rabid.

"Could someone be following us?" Brigit asked.

We all whipped our heads around. A faded yellow car trailed about eight car lengths back.

"That car has been behind us since we left the *casa*," Brigit said.

Even though I had no reason to watch for a tail, I was piqued that Brigit had noticed before I did. I was doubly annoyed that if someone was following us, he now knew that he'd been made.

When Oscar pulled up in front of a house, the squat sedan continued past us. We inspected it.

"That's not an American car," I said.

"Russian," Oscar said. "A Lada."

"The driver looks like a gypsy woman," Ingrid added.

"No passenger," Brigit said. "Maybe she's going to pick up a friend."

"Right," I said.

Oscar turned his head toward the house. "This is it. The address Jose gave me."

By the standards of the McMansions that sprang up where I lived, the white Italianate home was not large, but the gracious portico and columns suggested wealth and class in a way the big boxy structures back in Santa Cruz did not.

"Wait here." If Colette was about to receive an unexpected caller, it would be better if it were one woman, alone.

"*Como no.*" Oscar's "of course" had a petulant ring to it, as though he was offended, or maybe disappointed, or maybe had expected just such bossy orders from a Yankee imperialist.

I climbed from the car and opened a squeaky wrought iron gate. The walkway was deeply shaded by overgrown shrubbery. Something brushed my neck. I batted at it with my arm. Leaves rustled and a branch snapped. *Oh, great. The first thing I've done is damage the landscaping.*

The porch resounded under my steps. Light filtered through the transom and leaded glass of the door. I pressed the doorbell but didn't hear a ring. I tried again with my ear to the door but heard no sound. A shadowy figure, silent as a ghost, appeared behind the thick glass. The door popped open, and I almost stumbled into Colette Delvaux's arms.

I'd thought my plane outfit rather classy until Colette bridled in front of me in black linen slacks and crisp white blouse. Her feet, however, were bare, the nails a glistening red as though newly painted.

"*C'est vous!*"

"Yup. It's me. Carol Sabala. *Buenos días.*" I extended my hand.

She offered a limp-noodle clasp while staring over my shoulder to Oscar's car at the curb. Not covered by a hat, her thick auburn hair swept across her forehead in a short, stylish cut. Hair, or lack of it, made a person look so different. She said something in French.

"Translator." I pointed at the Chevy. "*Traductora*," I added in Spanish. One of the words must have resembled the French because she nodded.

I marched to the car and asked Ingrid to come with me.

"Why Ingrid?" Briget asked.

Ingrid slid from the vehicle. She and I both knew why it was Ingrid. Briget was her personal trainer. We didn't need a lengthy explanation or an argument to arrive at the inevitable conclusion of who called the shots. And I didn't want to overwhelm Colette with a cluster of people.

At the door Ingrid introduced herself to Colette. At the sound of fluent French, Colette's face softened, and she waved us into the house. Inside light fell on well-maintained marble floors, and a breeze blew through open French doors. The two women chatted briefly in the foyer before Colette motioned us into her living room. The rattan chair I chose was hard, but the ironwork sculptures distracted me from its stiffness.

"Lovely place," I said, and Ingrid promptly translated.

Colette smiled thinly and spoke.

"She says that you must be here about Megan Melquist."

I nodded.

Collette perched on a rattan settee and launched into animated French.

"Megan called her this morning about some strange man in line," Ingrid said. "She says that you know who she means. Megan asked if Collette knew where he was staying."

Excitement charged through me like I was a dog catching a scent. Why would Megan ask Colette about Aaron Phelps' location? Had she changed her mind about sharing a ride to the clinic in Jagüey? Aaron Phelps had told me that he'd given Megan his telephone number. Why wouldn't Megan just call him? Had she lost his number? How did she know the guy had been there? Who was this Aaron Phelps, anyway?

I looked at Ingrid, directly across from me in a chair that matched mine. "Was she able to tell Megan where Aaron Phelps is staying?"

"Hotel Ambos Mundos," Colette said before Ingrid translated.

My pulse quickened even as I wondered if Colette understood English, but simply refused to speak it. None of this meant Megan was going to Hotel Ambos Mundos. She probably would contact the guy via telephone. If she even did that. Aaron Phelp was pretty strange. Nonetheless, the connection was exciting.

I turned to Ingrid. "Ask her if she and Megan ever discussed favorite places—walks or dress shops. Bars. Music venues. Cafes."

CHAPTER TWENTY-EIGHT

The double shot espresso kick-started Megan's body. She reached down to untwist the white skirt from around her legs. A young couple strolling by on the street stared through the bistro's window at her almost bald head. Or maybe they gawked at her white clothing. She put a hand behind her head, elbow out, chin and chest up, like a preening fashion model. The pair looked back toward her, bumped shoulders, and laughed.

She opened the small beaded purse secured across her shoulder. Pawing aside the wad of CUC, she regarded the syringe and the vial of insulin—enough to be missed, but a small enough amount to stir self-doubt. The user would wonder if he'd lost count. After all, who would want to take those things?

The real question was whether it was enough to do the job. She'd have to get up close and personal, but that wouldn't be hard. Eric's ego created a huge blind spot. She'd convince him that she'd made a horrible mistake, that he *was* the love of her life, and she wanted to come back. She'd go to him in the late afternoon, when a person's blood sugar tended to be low.

She was glad that she didn't have to hit a vein. With insulin a person just stabbed into a part of the body. If she hiked up her skirt and lured him into a knee buckler, his butt would be completely exposed, a perfect target. His ankles would be shackled in his pants. If she wrapped her legs around his waist, made him take her weight, it would be a nice, sweaty work out for him, further depleting his sugar.

She zipped up the purse and drank her espresso. Her heart-beat accelerated. She swiped at perspiration along her temples. This was better than a rollercoaster.

CHAPTER TWENTY-NINE

"Shake our tail," I said.

"Huh?"

I'd gone beyond the bounds of Oscar's educated English.

Ingrid leaned over the seat. "She means try to lose the car behind us."

"The tail *I* spotted." Briget sulked in the corner of the back seat, refusing to be excited, angry that she'd been excluded from Colette's house.

Oscar sped up, and we careened around a corner.

"You almost hit him!" Briget gripped the back of my seat. A man on a bici-taxi wobbled, trying to regain his balance.

Oscar executed several quick turns down small streets. Pedestrians pressed against buildings as though car chases happened every day. The driver behind us reappeared around each corner with no problem. Oscar's Chevy wasn't fast to begin with, and now four bodies weighed it down. Plus it was easy to spot. The sedan nudged close. The driver was a woman with big hair springing from the bottom of a bright turquoise scarf.

"Who desires to follow you?" Ingrid asked.

"The million dollar question."

"She looks like a gypsy," Ingrid added.

"Stop!" I commanded.

Oscar slammed on his brakes, rocking us all forward. Briget yowled something in French. Our tail screeched to a halt ten feet behind us. I leapt from the taxi. Oscar, Briget and Ingrid followed suit. For one startled moment, the middle-aged woman in the Lada stared at us. With her painted red lips, big hoop earrings, and a billion bracelets on her forearms she looked more like a Halloween gypsy than a real gypsy.

By the time I touched the hood, she'd put the Lada in reverse and stepped on the gas. The car swerved its way back down the narrow street. This time the pedestrians jumped aside like they meant it. My whole posse was physically fit, but the driver was fearless. As we chased, the car bumped onto the sidewalk and rammed a pedal cart. Limes spilled over the concrete. The owner of the cart was off his bike and threw himself back against the wall. He shook his fist and cursed the gypsy driver. Limes rolled into our paths. We high-stepped through the obstacle course and closed the distance between the car and us to a matter of feet. Oscar and Ingrid split to the left and Briget and I to the right.

The car roared backward, the two tires on the sidewalk whamming back to the street. With her head twisted, the gypsy drove at full speed toward the corner. A car turned onto the street.

Yes!

Instead of cooperatively boxing in our quarry, the car reversed from the yellow juggernaut hurtling toward it. At the corner, the gypsy executed a brilliant three-point turn and sped away. When the four of us reached the intersection, we stood there huffing, the Lada already out of sight.

Still, when she'd hit the curb, I'd seen a head in the back pop up like a Jack-in-the-Box. The person wore a cap so the sighting didn't tell me much except the gypsy was just the driver. Weirdly, even from a distance, the design on the cap looked like the interlocking orange S and F of a San Francisco Giants baseball cap.

We trooped back toward the taxi. The pedal cart owner was busy picking up limes, but raised his head long enough to shout obscenities at us.

"Should I continue to the café?" Oscar asked when we reached his car.

"Yes. While I go inside, I want you all to keep a look out. I don't think we've scared them. Try to see the passenger."

None of the three asked about the existence of a passenger, so they must have caught a glimpse of the figure, too. What Giants fan could be here in Cuba and want to follow me? *Megan could be a Giants fan.* Or, could Lucille be so controlling that she'd sent someone to Cuba to monitor me? Could that be the role of the strange Aaron Phelps? Or how about Eric Mars, himself? The thought gave me chills.

Oscar's brakes were not exactly smooth. We lurched to a stop in front of Café Loco. I jumped out and the girls started to follow. "No," I said. "Just me."

The cafe proclaimed a new age for Havana. Behind a length of stainless steel, a shiny espresso machine hissed steam. Customers bellied up to the counter. Lightwood stools faced similar counters in front of the large windows. Framed abstract art decorated the available wall space. The aroma of coffee filled the air.

I ordered a cappuccino *para llevar*—to go—from the barista. A black tank top revealed her toned arms and the first tattoo I had seen in Cuba, a simple black line depiction of Che Guevara. I held up three photographs of Megan. *¿Ha visto a esta mujer?"* Have you seen this woman?

She frowned at the photos. "Maybe," she said in Spanish as

she cranked the scoop of espresso into position. "*¿Americana?*"

"Yes."

The barista patted her springy Afro. "But she doesn't have hair."

My heart thudded. "Yes. That's right."

"Is she your friend?"

"A good friend."

The young woman wrinkled her forehead and tugged an earlobe as though she knew that was unlikely. She lifted a lever to add steamed milk to the slurry of espresso and handed me the drink. "Two CUC."

I gave her the bills. She eyed my other bills.

I tweezered out a five CUC note.

She twisted her earlobe and shook her head.

I tried a twenty.

"She was here a moment ago."

"*¿Cómo un minuto?*" Like a minute? That didn't sound like correct Spanish, but my blood was pumping so fast, I would have been lucky to speak correct English. "Five minutes? What?"

"Maybe five."

"Which way did she go?"

The barista shrugged.

"What was she wearing?"

"White skirt. White blouse. Like a Santeria."

I hustled to the car, sloshing cappuccino across the top of my hand.

"Circle the block!" I licked foam from my wrist.

Oscar jolted into traffic and more hot coffee splashed onto the back of my hand. I barked an order to watch for a bald woman dressed in white. I hazarded my first drink of the cappuccino, the coffee rich, dark and satisfying, even with the milk. Oscar circled the block, all four of us scanning the streets for a bald woman in white.

We expanded the radius to two blocks, then three, then

four. I asked myself why I was doing this. Lucille had not hired me to capture her daughter. She'd said only to let her know she was alive. I could return to the U.S. and report that as of five minutes ago, Megan Melquist was alive. Yet I knew Lucille wanted more than that. She wanted a full report. She wanted me to meet with Megan, to find out how she was doing. In reality, Lucille hoped for the impossible. She wanted me to bring her daughter back.

As we searched for Megan, we didn't have to keep our eyes peeled for the yellow sedan. It had rejoined us on our way to the café and followed us as though tied to our bumper. Had Megan found out about me? Was she having me followed? A scarier thought seized me. I was in the country illegally. Was I under surveillance by undercover police?

With the coffee, my nerves, and the excitement of honing in on Megan's turf, every part of my body was wired. But none of us spotted Megan. And no one saw the passenger in the vehicle even though it trailed us like a can tied onto a Just Married car. Could Eric Mars be in Cuba?

CHAPTER THIRTY

Eric shook the mug until the scorpions reared up their tails. He chuckled. They were in fighting form, probably irritable from being cooped up in the cup. It didn't look like they'd eaten any of the dog food. They probably didn't eat much. Did they need water? He tried to remember if the terrariums at the clinic held troughs. It would suck if the creatures died before he could use them. Mug in hand, Eric used his free hand to turn on the bathroom tap. He rinsed his hand and with a wet index finger dripped water along the ceramic walls. When he wiggled the cup again, the scorpions scrabbled at the edges. Satisfied, he stretched the latex glove back over the top.

Eric sat the scorpions on the nightstand and paced to the slatted French door, which folded like an accordion. There was no balcony, just a decorative ledge that ran below the fifth-floor rooms. He could step right out there and view the city. He snorted. In the United States the hotel would be required to have a rail, and it better be the right height, too, so if some moron went out there and fell off, the hotel couldn't be sued.

The breeze buffeted his bare head and he ran his palm over his scalp. The stubble was already long enough to have lost its prickliness. In no time, he'd have his hair back. Short and spiky would be fun to try for a while. Would Megan like his new look? He'd tell her he had shaved his hair in solidarity with her. She'd eat that shit up. He imagined her eyes dewy, her face soft as a little girl's at the idea he'd joined in her struggle. Megan had been trying all her life to get someone to see her. Hell, she couldn't even see her friggin' self. She was a scared girl hiding in a closet waiting for someone to discover her. Not just find her—rescue her and whisk her off on big, bold adventures. She wanted all that while she hid inside her shell and barricaded herself with a noisy bar. It took someone like him to punch through barriers like that.

Eric flicked his hands to shake off energy. He closed the louvered doors and pulled shut the gauzy drapes. The rush from thoughts about Megan was like coke. He felt energized and powerful. He whirled at the sound of footsteps in the hallway. Voices seeped into his room. A whole group of people. He'd asked for a top-floor room with a view, expecting privacy. He slipped on his loafers and cracked his door. Five people, talking in hushed voices in some foreign language, paraded from the elevator to a room two doors down. Once they entered the room, Eric prowled down the hallway.

A plaque outside the door showed a face designated as Ernest Hemingway. He should have seen this and known it would be a problem. He'd been so pumped with the success of the day that he'd been careless. While he hadn't found Megan, he now knew her café, and once Megan found something she liked, she held on to it like a security blanket. The way she did with Brittany.

As he examined the Spanish words under Hemingway's face, a burning sensation flared up in his stomach, replacing the glee he'd felt. He was two rooms away from a tourist trap! Even if the tourists didn't pass his room, he couldn't have people riding up and down in the elevator to his floor, swarming the hallway.

He panted, struggling to gain control of a fire spreading in his pit. This old sensation didn't burble up often anymore, but he recognized it as the prelude to losing control. Anxiety percolated to the edges of his skin. He pressed a hand into Hemingway's face to brace himself and closed his eyes. That made it worse. The Mickey Mantle card flashed behind his eyelids, a series of them, like a deck fanned by an expert dealer, all with the cigarette burn, right in the center.

When he'd seen his precious card on the coffee table like that, he'd lunged like an animal, even though his mom was barely conscious in front of the television. He'd charged with such force he bowled over her chair. His mom, drunk and protected by the cushion, grunted awake, while he rammed his head into the wall. A lump swelled on his forehead, and he saw double, so he knew he was concussed.

"You'll live," his mom had said. She crawled out of the lounger, shouldered it upright, and lit a cigarette. "Put some ice on it." She never even asked why he'd attacked her.

The hotel door in front of him opened, and a young woman peered out. "I thought I heard someone."

Eric pulled away from the Hemingway plaque.

"Are you all right?"

He smiled. "I'm much better now." Even though the young woman wore tights, her legs were mighty fine below the short skirt of her uniform.

"Are you here for the tour?"

"Sure."

After he followed the woman's ass into the room, she explained to the group that the table under a manual Remington typewriter could be raised and lowered. "Hemingway could not write for long periods seated in a chair," she said in careful English, "due to wounds sustained in World War I."

As the guide directed the attention of the three women and two men toward the bed, Eric moved around the perimeter.

"This room was Hemingway's first residence in Cuba," the guide said.

Eric stopped for a moment by a model of a boat made from various woods. Hemingway's boat, the Pilar. Interesting what rich and famous meant back then. A lot of ordinary people had nicer boats in the Santa Cruz Harbor.

A bureau displayed a Decca record and a photograph of a stole-draped movie star.

Eric remembered what the receptionist had told him about some woman climbing along the face of the building to get into Hemingway's room. The guy must have gotten a lot of action.

With that thought, he slipped out of the room.

CHAPTER THIRTY-ONE

The cab driver dropped Megan around the corner from Hotel Ambos Mundos. She stood across the street from the hotel and ran her eyes up the side of the familiar building. Between her visits to the Duarte's, when she'd felt well enough, she'd had a lot of time to kill. She'd toured all the Hemingway sites, his house Finca Vigía, rotting away on a plot of overgrown jungle, tarps thrown over what must have been invaluable items. She'd visited El Cobre to see Papa's Nobel Prize medal at the shrine to Our Lady of Charity, Cuba's patron saint—a sort of Caribbean version of the Virgin Mary. She'd thrown her arms around the neck of the Hemingway statue at the Floridita and had toured room 511 here at Hotel Ambos Mundos.

Had she subconsciously chosen Cuba because Hemingway had chosen it? Her favorite course in college had been one that focused on Steinbeck, Fitzgerald and Hemingway. She wished she'd lived a big bold life like they had. Hemingway had created something new and original. Her heart panged at the utter waste of her thirty-two years.

She bit her lip and crossed the street. Walking along Obispo, she looked for the right kind of store, a place that sold candy bars. Just in case things went sideways and Eric got the drug away from her—injected her. She started to despair. This was not a street littered with convenience stores. At one small grocery store, she tried to explain what she meant. Hershey's and Snickers elicited blank stares from the young girl at the counter. The clerk called to an older boy in the aisle. They had a discussion and came to some sort of agreement, shaking their heads at her.

Finally, she spotted a hole-in-the-wall ice cream vendor. No cones—just a kind of ice cream sandwich. She ordered two and gobbled them down. It wasn't hard. Other than Cuban coffee, they were the best things she'd tasted in weeks.

She headed toward the hotel, wanting now to hurry, but the long white skirt grabbed at her legs. She had not changed her clothing because this seemed like a bad time to piss off the gods.

On the threshold of the hotel, small mosaic tiles spelled out Hotel Ambos Mundos. Overhead, flags fluttered. She stood there and scanned the lobby and bar. She looked back over her shoulder.

"Is everything okay, miss?" the doorman asked.

She nodded and crossed the lobby to the back.

At reception, the young woman asked, "How may I help you?"

Megan gulped. She placed her small beaded bag on the counter and took a deep breath. "Could you tell me if Eric Mars is staying here?" Then she added, "He may also be using the name Aaron Phelps."

The young woman froze. The smile vanished. Her eyes scoured Megan.

What was this? Had Eric slept with this woman? She was very pretty, but looked about twenty. Not that that would stop Eric.

"Excuse me," the receptionist said. "This may take a moment. Please take a seat in the lobby."

Megan swiveled to inspect the lobby. Her heart thudded. Clearly Eric was in the hotel. Right now. And something was up. She'd hoped that he would be here, and yet part of her wanted to grab her purse and run. Instead she looped the straps around her neck and over her shoulder like an old lady, afraid of a purse-snatcher. She licked her lips. They were dry and chapped.

"Please, if you would wait there." The woman gestured toward the lobby.

Megan staggered to a cluster of couches and collapsed. *What if Eric had moved on? What if she could no longer entice him?* He would still want revenge on her for leaving, but she'd be approaching him with no advantage at all.

Megan stood so that she could see the receptionist talking intently into the phone. The woman glanced her way and Megan knew. This woman was not going to help her. The receptionist was reporting her to someone. Megan opened the purse. Her fingers trembled as she pushed aside the bills on top. She looked about for the lobby restroom.

At the sink Megan stuck the needle into the ampule and watched the insulin suck into the syringe. She capped the needle, placed the full syringe in her purse and slid into the lobby. The steps to the upper floors were tucked out of the receptionist's sight line. Megan climbed the first flight before pressing the call button for the elevator. Eric could be unpredictable, but he would be on the top floor. He always wanted to be on top.

CHAPTER THIRTY-TWO

Oscar sped toward Hotel Ambos Mundos. He was in a sour mood because I'd told him I'd already eaten lunch.

To lose the tail, I'd had him drop Briget, Ingrid and me at Casa Maria. It had been past two, and the girls and I had been famished. We'd decided to eat Maria's black bean soup at the *casa*. During the meal, I told them that I would be continuing my investigation on my own. They both stopped slurping their soup.

Briget gave me a downturned mouth. Ingrid glared. "We came all the way from Viñales to be sleuths for one morning?"

"Briget said you were planning to come to Havana anyway."

Ingrid switched her glare to Briget.

I got up from the table and walked to the balcony to see if Oscar had returned. When I'd paid him for the midday trip, I had requested, under my breath, that he return to the *casa* at three.

He showed up promptly as though he'd been waiting nearby for the three o'clock hour. When I climbed into the cab, he asked me straight off, "Lunch?"

"No. I ate in the *casa*. Please take me to El Floridita."

While I went into the bar, Oscar stormed off somewhere to eat, on his own dime. The bartender recognized me from the morning. There were customers at the bar but when I approached, he turned away. Embarrassed, I guessed, for being such a dick earlier. With a bar to attend, he couldn't keep his back to me forever. I placed a twenty CUC bill on the counter. Bartenders had peripheral vision, honed for such movement. He turned slightly.

"Tonic water."

"Ice?"

"Please. *Con limón*." The word might mean lemon, but I expected, as in Mexico, to receive lime.

When he delivered the drink with a wedge of lime, I slid the bill to him along with a photograph of Megan. "Have you seen this woman?"

He shrugged.

"You can keep the change."

He picked up the money and then scrutinized the photo. "Sure."

"When?"

"I don't know. A few weeks ago."

"Just once?"

"Yeah."

"What did she do?"

"The usual tourist stuff. Had Joey there," he nodded toward a helper, "take a photo of her with Hemingway." He aimed his chin at the bronze statue in the corner. "Then she ordered a Papa doble."

"What's that?"

"Supposedly what Hemingway drank—a daiquiri with double the rum and no sugar."

"But she hasn't been back?"

"Not that I know of."

"Has Joey seen her since then?"

The bartender snapped his fingers. Joey sat down a tray of empties and hustled over. The bartender flipped the photo in his face and repeated the question in Spanish. The kid shook his head.

Another strike out.

Now Oscar barreled toward Hotel Ambos Mundos. He sulked, not talking to me. I planned to see if Megan had contacted the strange Aaron Phelps since she'd asked Colette about the man's 'location.'

At the side of the hotel, Oscar slammed on his brakes, throwing me forward. "Here you are."

"I'm not sure how long this will take."

"Take as long as you want. I have other business."

When I got out of the car, he executed a U turn, and roared down the street, his car belching smoke.

He was really ticked about lunch.

CHAPTER THIRTY-THREE

When Eric answered his room phone, the receptionist whispered, "I think your stalker is here."

"Don't worry." He relaxed back on the bed, planting his loafers on the bedspread. "Tell her I'm out." He would order room service and chill. Eventually, Carol Sabala would get tired and bail. There was no reason to talk to her now. Thanks to Sabala, he would find Megan soon enough. He had returned to the café, worked his magic with the barista, and knew it was Megan's regular spot. Just like that. He snapped his fingers.

He rubbed under his bottom lip, getting used to the new, smooth feel without the soul patch. At this point, he could hardly reappear as Aaron Phelps. There was no small pillow in the room to stick in his pants and he didn't have any gum to wedge into his mouth. None of that mattered. He had no reason to reappear as Aaron Phelps—no reason to talk to Carol Sabala. If things didn't work out tomorrow, he would hire

Alvina, the gypsy, to follow her again, see if the investigator got even closer to Megan, but—nah—Aaron Phelps was dead.

"She seems intent on waiting." For all her training, Eric heard the insecurity of the receptionist's youth.

"Let her wait." The detective had work to do, a missing person to track down. She wouldn't spend her whole evening waiting for him. He had hoped to go down and change his room, but that would have to wait until after she was gone.

"I think she knows you are here," the receptionist said.

The girl's voice dripped with worry. "It's okay, sweetheart. Just don't tell her my room number."

"I won't. She seems very nervous, though."

Nervous? He almost laughed. That didn't sound at all like the woman he'd met. The girl was letting her imagination run wild. "She's not dangerous," he said.

There was a pause. "She's disappeared." The receptionist let out a long exhale, clearly relieved.

"Thank you for the warning," Eric said. "You've been terrific." He smiled to himself. That had been easy. Carol Sabala here and gone just like that. "Now speaking of my room number, this Hemingway museum thing up here is a problem. Do you have something quiet on the fourth floor?"

While he waited for her to check, he extracted the Minnie Miñoso card from a travel brochure where he'd stuck it for protection. The card was truly a thing of beauty—original color and gloss.

"We have a nice corner room," the woman said. "You'd be right below the Hemingway room and have much the same view."

"Don't give the room to anyone else," he said. "I'll be down in a while to make the change. Are you sure my stalker left?"

"One moment." He heard the phone clunk on to a surface. While he waited, he toyed with the price he'd ask for the Minnie Miñoso. The collector jones-ing for the card was a Miami Cuban. Forty years, and his heart was still stuck here.

Eric couldn't see it. What was so great about this shitty island? Well, what did he care? The guy's nostalgia was good for him. He figured he could get a thousand bucks for the card. It filled a hole in the dude's collection. *A hole in his soul.* Eric chuckled at his rhyme.

The receptionist came back on the line. "I looked in the lobby and the bar. I don't see her."

"Thank you," he said. "You are *the best.*"

After he put down the phone, he thought about the card that he'd sold before the trip, the 1951 Bowman #305 card—four perfect edges, exactly centered, good color. But that memory led to the little schoolteacher. His failure to get an erection. Rage burbled up in him and propelled him off the bed.

He paced to the French doors, and threw back the flimsy drapes. He couldn't believe his eyes.

CHAPTER THIRTY-FOUR

When Megan had entered room 511, the docent was saying to a tour group, "Hemingway wrote the first chapters of *For Whom the Bell Tolls* in this room." Her eyes lit with recognition, and the docent waved Megan into the room. "You have returned." It was no wonder the girl remembered her from a month ago. Megan had asked about a million questions.

The guide's smile disappeared and her head pulled back as she took in Megan's clothing. "We have almost finished the tour."

Perfect.

"It's the last one of the day," she added.

There were five people in the group with the docent. The room felt crowded, which was good.

Megan hung at the fringes, backing toward the louvered doors to the tiny balcony. The doors were folded inward so tourists could admire Hemingway's view of the city, over rooftops and trees all the way to the sea. She waited until the group neared the exit to the hallway. The guide stopped to point out the model of Hemingway's boat.

Megan stepped through the opening to a narrow balcony, more decorative than functional. A person might stand there, but the thick posts and rail took up most of the space. Certainly a chair wouldn't fit.

The tour guide whipped around. "What are you doing?"

Megan swallowed. "I don't feel well. I need some air."

The statement was truer than she'd intended.

The guide crossed the room. "Do you feel faint?"

Megan nodded. She did, in spite of all the sugar she'd consumed.

One of the male tourists also approached and fussed with the doors, folding them more widely open over the patterned floor, as though that could help in some way. Megan leaned into the fresh air and inhaled deeply. "Thank you. I feel much better." She fanned her face with a hand. "I get these spells from my chemo." Their eyes softened with sympathy. They didn't question her lie. "Please don't let me interfere with your tour. I'll be fine now."

She could tell they were concerned, but they didn't want to embarrass her, and they were probably glad not to deal with an emergency. The docent motioned the man back to the model of the Pilar. "Hemingway acquired his fishing boat for $7,495 in April 1934 from Wheeler Shipbuilding in Brooklyn, New York."

"How big was it?" asked the man who had fiddled with the French doors. Megan couldn't place the accent of their English. *Eastern European?*

"Thirty-eight feet, or twelve meters." The docent replied as though proud to know such minutia. She pointed to the Spanish language copies of Hemingway's books in the case below.

Megan shuffled to the side of the narrow balcony. The slatted doors partially blocked her view of the group—and vice versa, she hoped. She peeked at the group. They all angled toward the bookcase.

A woman pointed. "What is that one?"

The tour guide squatted. "Which one?"

The other four leaned toward the books.

"Oh that," the guide said. "*Ho guardato il cielo e la terra.* That book was written by Adriana Ivancich, a young woman with whom Hemingway was enamored."

As the guide shepherded the group to the exterior door, Megan climbed over the rail to the ledge. She was, as her favorite oxymoron put it: *freely committed.* A mountain climber could only hope for such a substantial ledge—probably two feet wide, plenty of room for her feet and body. She shuffled sideways. A breeze caressed her face. She pressed her palms against the prickly exterior of the building. It felt almost like natural rock, warm, with a sandstone smell to it. She felt the rush that made her love climbing.

Her clothing, though, was not climbing gear. The skirt twisted around her legs. Pressed to the pink stucco, she crabbed along the wall. She didn't have much time. The tour guide would soon discover her absence. If the guide didn't sound the alarm, the people below, across the street, could see her and might alert the police. On the other hand, she was scuttling along, face to the wall. She would not look like someone planning to jump. Spectators might think she was an act, like the mimes that performed on the sidewalk.

She arrived at the next set of French doors. Only the corner rooms like Hemingway's had rails to create a tiny balcony. But that was good—no obstacles to climb over. Diaphanous drapes were pulled across the doors, but they didn't meet in the center. She peeped through the crack. This room was empty. That made sense. *Who would want to stay in the room next to a tourist mecca?* Certainly not Eric Mars.

Logically, to find Eric, she should have walked down the hallway pounding on the doors. But there was nothing daring or bold about that. Out here on the ledge she felt exhilarated. The air was fresh up here, full of the smell of the sea. She felt alive like before the drop on a roller coaster.

"What are you doing?" the tour guide shrieked.

Megan did not turn her head, but the voice came from outside the room. "Don't worry. I'm just traveling to another room."

"Are you crazy?"

"Jane Mason did it." Jane Mason had supposedly walked this very ledge to gain access to Hemingway's room. "Was she crazy?"

"Well, actually," the tour guide said, "she probably was. She didn't jump from this ledge, but she did jump from the balcony of her house."

"I'm not going to jump," Megan said, continuing to move. She could not waste time with chitchat. On the other hand, as long as the guide was talking, she was not calling the management. Perhaps the rotary dial phone in the museum room was a prop. "My boyfriend is in the next room." *Or the next.* "I want to surprise him." *Nothing like the truth, or sort of truth.*

The guide didn't respond. Megan sensed that she'd left. She inched along the wall. *Thank God this was not a gigantic hotel.* Her skirt whipped in the breeze and wrapped around her left leg. She stopped, stretched down a hand and unfurled it. The fabric caught in the breeze and billowed outward like an angel's wing.

CHAPTER THIRTY-FIVE

I turned the corner to the front of Hotel Ambos Mundos. Across Obispo Street, a crowd was dispersing. The mimes were not performing in front of the building, so I wondered what the small swarm had been watching. Aaron Phelps could wait a moment. I crossed Obispo and approached a couple walking away from the knot of people. "What happened?" I asked in English. A camera dangled from the woman's wrist so I assumed they were tourists.

"A woman was up there." The man pointed toward the top of the building and the woman's gaze followed the trajectory of his finger.

"A jumper?"

The man shrugged bony shoulders under a crisp white dress shirt. Red suspenders and gray fedora gave him a dated, urbane appearance. "Well, she didn't jump." With knobby fingers, he straightened wire rim glasses.

"I don't think she ever meant to jump," the woman piped up.

I turned my attention to her, a silver-haired lady, who spoke English with softened edges. Her native tongue was Spanish, or something similar. She, too, was dressed up by American standards, sporting a tweedy jacket and skirt, although her dark gray shoes were sensible for walking. "What was the woman doing on the roof?" I asked them.

"Not the roof," the man said. "She was on the ledge."

I ran my eyes along the decorative outcropping below the fifth-floor rooms. A niggly crawled up my spine. I returned my attention to the couple. "If she wasn't thinking about suicide, what was she doing there?"

The man smiled. "She apparently was taking an adventurous route from one room to another." He wiggled his gray eyebrows.

I glanced up again.

"It looked like a romantic rendezvous." The woman's smile was much fuller. "Romeo and Juliet."

"Why do you say that?" I asked, studying her face.

"A man came to the door and pulled her in."

"How could you see all that?" the man asked the woman. His querulous tone cemented my assumption that they were husband and wife.

The woman shot a withering look up at him. "I was going to take a photo." She swiveled toward me. "I zoomed in."

"Did you take the photo?"

"No." The woman made a disappointed tsk sound. "She disappeared before I could focus."

"What a strange event," I said.

"I'll say." The man twisted his wrist and checked a round gold watch. "Excuse us." He looked at his wife. "We are ten minutes late."

By the time the couple walked away, the rubberneckers had disappeared. I didn't see any police. Perhaps they'd already been there and heard the same story—some crazy lover high jinks. Nothing to worry about. But the silver-haired lady's comment about Romeo and Juliet compounded my anxiety.

I crossed the street, entered Hotel Ambos Mundos, and made my way back to the reception counter. A different, much younger woman looked up at me.

"*Buenas tardes.*" I thought using Spanish would increase good will.

She greeted me and asked how she might help.

"I am here to meet a friend. Could you tell me if Aaron Phelps has checked in?"

She did not look down at her registry. Instead she scrutinized my face.

"Is something wrong?" I asked.

"You are looking for Aaron Phelps? The writer?"

"Yes." I guessed I was. How many Aaron Phelps could there be in Cuba? *A writer*. That explained his peculiarity.

The young woman tapped her pen on the counter. "Could I see some identification?"

"Certainly." Something was not right. I shifted from foot to foot, a sense of unease growing inside me. I handed her my passport and business card.

She opened the passport with trembling fingers and compared my photo to my face. She glanced at my business card. "You are a private investigator?"

"Yes."

"Is Aaron Phelps in trouble?"

"Do you think he could be?"

"I need to call him."

"Okay. I can wait."

She spun away from me, punched a number on the phone, and waited. After a moment she said, "He's not picking up."

"But you think he should be picking up?"

The girl compressed her lips and frowned. She leaned forward and scouted the room for help, but the women who sat at the desks for tour information had closed shop and the doorman had stepped outside the entrance.

It's just you and me, baby. I waited her out, forcing myself to remain motionless, to appear calm. Most people dreaded a vortex of silence. I expected this to be doubly true for a person in the hospitality industry.

"This is such a bizarre coincidence. You are the second woman to come looking for him today," she babbled. "He told me he had *a* stalker. One." She held up a forefinger to emphasize the fact of one, and only one.

"I'm not a stalker." I kept my voice level. The girl was tentative. Her eyes scanned my face as if to detect a sinister scar or secret microchip.

"You don't look like a stalker," she said.

"How about the other woman? Did she?"

The nod was infinitesimal. The girl glanced back into the office, even though no one was there. She bent over the counter and peered toward the doorman, but he was watching passersby on the sidewalk. "Yes," she whispered. "She looked crazy."

My thoughts were running wild—*crazy, the woman on the ledge, Aaron Phelps. Aaron Phelps who was at the* Duarte's. *Here. At a place Megan had visited. Aaron Phelps who'd looked familiar. Aaron Phelps with the shaved off hair and make up on his face. Could it be?* Anxiety buzzed through my body. I took a deep breath. I had to stay cool to maintain the fragile connection with this young woman.

"How did she look?"

"Sweaty. Nervous."

"Was she tall with no hair?"

"That was her!"

My heart hammered. "Please," I said, "what's his room number?"

CHAPTER THIRTY-SIX

Eric blinked.

But the figure was not an apparition. Outside the slats, a woman stood, dressed in white, like an angel plopped down from heaven. He tugged open the flimsy doors. *Megan!* Her hands hiked up the front of her skirt and she pressed slender naked thighs toward him. She had come to him. His power had returned. He yanked her into the room.

Her arms wrapped around his neck and she kissed his throat. "I've missed you so much."

Heat coursed through him like he'd had a shot of good whiskey. Her musk scent made him dizzy. He reached up to loosen the grip around his neck, but she held on as though she had suction cups on her arms. For someone sick, she sure was strong. "I missed you, too, babe," he whispered. "Why else do you think I came all the way to Cuba?"

"I was crazy to run away."

She released one hand voluntarily and it traveled right to his cock. At her touch, the old magic returned, like she was some kind of witch. She knew exactly how much squeeze he liked. He kept his eyes open and pushed her shoulder to back her off, so he could see what she was doing.

"What's with the white get-up?" he asked. "You look like one of those Santeria girls."

She kept one arm locked around his neck. The other hand moved up to undo the button above his fly. She didn't answer.

"I guess you like my cue-ball look?" he said.

"You look great with any haircut." She murmured into his ear. She added tongue. It excited him as much as getting sucked off.

He unzipped his jeans for her. "I shaved my head to be like you. Solidarity and all that. Show the world we belong together."

"That's why I love you, Eric."

She was lapping it up, like he knew she would. The Big L word, even. Megan wasn't the type to throw it around. In the end, though, she was just another bitch like his mother, pretending to care, snaring him and then deserting him, screwing up his world. He put both hands on her shoulders and pressed down. Without resistance, she knelt beneath his power. She worked his pants and underwear down his legs. His cock sprang free. God, he was hard as a steel rod. She gave it a kiss and a lick. He was getting into it, when she rose to her feet.

He preferred a blowjob, but she pulled up her skirt again and backed against the wall. The bad girl seduction worked for him, and this would be an easier position for throwing her onto the bed. He couldn't wait to pin her and pour the scorpions onto her pale flesh, to feel her body tighten and to see her eyes stretch wide. He pushed the thought away so he wouldn't explode too soon. That would ruin everything. He needed to last until those scorpions thrust their stingers into her. Then he would shoot his wad onto her face.

She was smiling at him. Even chapped, her lips were perfect—not puffed up with collagen or thin like a hag's. Her eyes weren't doe-like, though. They looked weird—shimmery, like she was tripping on something. He watched her unzip her purse. *What was that about? A condom?* He'd never used one and wasn't about to start. But her hand lifted, empty, away from the beaded bag. She sucked on the tip of her finger, touched her clit and beckoned him forward.

He bent down to slip off his loafers.

"Don't," she said. "Come as you are."

CHAPTER THIRTY-SEVEN

As Megan watched Eric hobble toward her, a sharp ache stabbed up from her heart. It had nothing to do with her cancer and everything to do with the way he trusted her, the way he believed he was in control. He placed his palms against the wall, and bent his knees to shove into her, as she knew he would. Underneath his bullying and hard muscles, was nothing but a damaged little boy, a kid with a cruel, alcoholic mother, and a father who never gave a shit about him. Eric was a guy who lucked into wealth and never learned to be accountable to the world. She'd seen all of this and had still cared about him, and that had frightened him, or angered him, or confused him. *Who the fuck knew what went on inside of Eric?*

She lifted one leg and wrapped it around his slim hip. He followed her cue and lowered his arms to take her weight in his hands. He thrust and banged her against the wall. The blow knocked the wind out of her and rattled a framed painting.

Had she forgotten how strong he was, or had she grown as insubstantial as a dry leaf? He rammed into her again. She reached for her purse. He spun, lifting her like a baby, the purse flying away from her fingers. Her plan twirled from her. He shuffled toward the bed. He meant to plop her on it. If he got on top, it was game over.

She dropped her legs, jarring him out of her. Shackled by his pants, he stumbled, off balance.

"God, Megan!" He bent and grabbed himself.

Her skirt tumbled around her legs as her hand thrust toward her purse. He straightened, snatched her purse straps, and crossed them. They cinched tight across her throat. Her hands fluttered up, scrabbling at the straps.

"What do you have in there?"

She tried to swallow and couldn't. "Something fun." She smiled at him.

"Oh, yeah?" The choking straps loosened a notch. "I have something fun, too." His eyes flicked toward a mug on the nightstand covered by a latex glove.

"Whisky?" She tried to smile again, but it was difficult with the beaded straps cutting off her air. "Neat?" She wanted him to think about her as a bartender, the way she was when they met.

"Noooo," he said. "Something better."

Holding the crisscrossed straps occupied both his hands and his pants bound his ankles. With the element of surprise, she could push him over, but she'd go with him. She would land on top, but he'd have a chokehold on her neck. She needed to talk her way out of this, even though she had no skilled patter, and at the moment could hardly breathe. "Not as good as what I have." She licked her lips and stared into his green eyes. They had none of their original hypnotic effect. They lightened like the eyes of a child promised candy.

"You scored coke?" The stranglehold relaxed a bit.

"Better."

"Better than coke?" His eyes glinted with suspicion.

She worried that she'd overplayed her hand. Her fingers inched toward the purse.

The straps tightened around her neck.

"Just let me show you."

The beads stopped cutting. His hands slammed into her solar plexus. She grunted and saw black with stars as she tumbled back onto the bed. Her head smacked the headboard.

"I can look for myself." He sat his weight on her thighs.

She blinked and her vision returned, but the room spun. One of Eric's hands crushed her breast as he stretched across her toward the purse. After wanting desperately to breathe, she now held her breath.

Beside her on the nightstand, something scratched inside the mug.

CHAPTER THIRTY-EIGHT

The young receptionist stared at me, her brow wrinkled. "I promised not to give out his room number."

"That was because of his stalker, right?" I glanced toward the grillwork door of the old elevator. The cage was not at the bottom. It could take forever for the elevator to arrive. The stairs must be in the corner of the lobby behind the doorman. He had returned to his post. "I'm not the stalker." I strained to keep my voice even, and maybe it sounded okay to a stranger, but I heard the edge of panic. "If you don't tell me the number, I think something really bad is going to happen."

"He told me the stalker was not dangerous." Her gaze darted about the room, searching for backup.

"Yes, but you told me she looked sweaty and nervous."

"But she left."

"Okay. But do you know where she went?"

"I have to check with the manager."

"Okay."

She moved to the back of the office, but glanced over her shoulder. The moment she was out of sight, I bent over the counter and snapped up the registry book. In two seconds I spotted what I feared—a scrawled signature, almost illegible, except for the big flourish on the E and the M. I dropped the book back into place and sprinted toward the steps. I should have maintained my composure.

The doorman turned to give me a curious look, stepped over to the marble stairs, and stretched out an arm like a barricade.

"*Despacio,*" he said, and then in English, "More slow."

"*Sí, sí, como no.*" I said to reassure him. When he lowered his arm, I took three steps in a civilized fashion and then bounded up the steps, two at a time.

Someone had told me Cuban workers all received the same subsistence level salary, whether a janitor or a doctor, so no one was particularly motivated to go beyond the call of duty. This doorman was an exception. He gave chase.

I had a head start and my calves were strong from mountain bike riding, but the guy was young and long legged. I reached the first landing with him right behind me. One lunge and he could tackle me, but he simply continued his pursuit. He must have had reservations about injuring a tourist.

"*¡Despacio!*"

What a ridiculous command when the guy was running as fast as I was.

I turned the corner to the next flight of stairs, sliding on slick marble. I raced up the steps with him huffing behind me. I hated to do it, but on the landing I stopped. As the young guy leapt up the final step, beaming triumphantly, I stuck out my foot. He sailed forward onto his hands.

The one second break allowed me to catch my breath. I sprinted to the next floor.

CHAPTER THIRTY-NINE

As Eric pulled the syringe from Megan's purse, he saw her glance at the mug. His torso snapped upright and his left hand snatched her wrist. "That's for later." He nudged the cup away from her reach. He held the syringe aloft. "What have we here?"

Her eyes were following the needle. He was fully erect and the rush of excitement was almost too much. *This was better than anything he could have planned, better than his best fantasy.*

"Heroin," she said.

"Oh, really?" *How in the hell could she have gotten heroin when he couldn't even score coke?* He eyed the clear liquid. "Not some weird voodoo potion?"

She shook her head. "Heroin. Cooked and ready to go."

"Someone has become a very bad girl."

"I've never used it."

Her thighs squished under his weight, her bones hard against his butt. No squirming or struggle. She was just watching him. He shifted his butt on to her lap to try to get comfortable, but his pants restricted the bottom of his legs. With his shoes on, his feet couldn't flex. They felt numb.

"I brought it for you." He heard her coaxing. "A present."

"Lift your head."

She raised her head a couple of inches like that was all she could manage. He wiggled the purse strap over her head. She was wearing the damn thing like some tourist who thought she'd be mugged. Once he had the strap over her head, he pulled it down to her elbow. "Presents are meant to be shared." He smiled at her. "You brought a perfect tie-off, too. Very thoughtful. Cinch it up like a good girl."

Her trembling hands complied. Each grabbed a strap, crossed it over pale skin, and pulled tight. He didn't have experience with needle drugs, but he'd had his blood drawn. It didn't seem that hard. He slapped the bend in her arm to raise a vein. A nice greenish-blue lump popped up in the crease. He touched it with the tip of the needle and watched her eyes.

CHAPTER FORTY

The cold needle touched Megan's inner elbow. Eric studied her face. She knew he wanted to see her cringe, to feel his power. She concentrated on Obatala, her orisha. Teasingly, he swiped the needle back and forth.

She wanted to laugh at the puny needle. It was nothing compared to the ones she'd seen in chemo—injecting her with all kinds of shit. This was nothing. She didn't know what the insulin might do to her. If it came to that, she hoped the ice cream sugar load would offset the effect.

But it wasn't going to come to that. A trance-like calm descended on her. She was the daughter of Obatala, the orisha of creation. She was bold. She'd walked out on a ledge to get here.

She waited. When the needle swept to the side of her elbow, she dropped the strap, lurched, and rammed the needle into his thigh. In the second before he could react, she pushed the plunger.

He sprang off her, the syringe dangling from his thigh, his erection wilted. "You fucking cunt." He yanked out the needle. Half the liquid was gone.

In one smooth motion, she grabbed the mug and rolled off the opposite side of the bed.

Across the bed, he raised his arm, holding up the hypodermic. He watched her peel off the latex glove. "No, no, no," he said.

"Oh." She smiled. "What a nice little present for me."

She picked up the mug and crawled up on the bed. He backed away.

"Don't do that, Megan."

She stood on the bed and bounced closer to him.

He waved the syringe at her.

"I'm not afraid of that." She'd lost count of the number of injections she'd received. The bruises from bad needle sticks on her inner arm. Nausea that wracked her body. "That's just a half dose of insulin."

"Insulin?"

"You think I'd waste heroin on you?" Rising, she took aim, thrust the mug forward, and pitched the two scorpions right on top his bald head.

CHAPTER FORTY-ONE

I ran down the fifth floor hallway, my athletic shoes slapping the floor. The doorman pounded right behind me. My extended foot had barely slowed his progress. *Damn the young!*

The phone shrilled inside Eric Mar's room. Probably the front desk calling to warn him that another crazy woman was on her way up. But no one was answering. I tried the knob. *Thank God for the old-fashioned hotel doors—no swipe required.*

Whatever tryst was happening, Eric had not bothered to lock the door. It flew open.

"*¡Pare!*"

The doorman was a little late with his command to stop. He lurched to a halt right behind me. I gaped at the scene in the room, and the doorman must have been doing the same because he didn't try to remove me from the entrance. He stood behind me breathing hard from the chase up four flights of stairs. He didn't utter a word.

The phone stopped ringing. Beside the bed, Eric stood, frozen, with his pants dropped around his ankles and a Hawaiian shirt fluttering open around an impressive torso. He didn't turn his head to see who had burst into his room. In high relief against his shiny scalp, two scorpions crawled, the bigger one about to go over the edge of the dome. A hypodermic needle half full of clear liquid rested beside his shoes.

In white clothing, Megan Melquist kneeled on the rumpled bedspread. She twisted toward us, her mouth in a startled O. She clutched a latex glove in one hand and a mug in the other.

I tried to figure out what all this could mean—the uses for the various objects. *What was in the syringe and had it been used for pleasure? Eric looked half-erect, but the scorpions didn't seem like an aphrodisiac. And Megan—what was she even doing here? She should be running the opposite direction from Eric Mars.* My mind failed to piece together the information.

"Don't move," Eric commanded. Whether to us or to Megan, I wasn't sure. "If you frighten the scorpions, they'll sting me." His voice was even and his body tranquil—eerily calm.

"You mean like this?" Megan rose to her feet and bounced across the bed. Using the mug, she tapped the large scorpion over the edge of Eric's scalp onto his shoulder.

The creature raised its stinger and scuttled over the ukulele pattern of the Hawaiian shirt's collar and onto Eric's neck. I stayed where I was, thinking of how Eric had deceived me with his Aaron Phelps charade. I was not sure I cared if the duplicitous bastard got stung.

Eric locked his head in a tilted position. "Shhhhh," he said, as though hushing a baby. "It's okay."

We all watched as he lifted his hand. It rose as slowly as water filling a sink. The open palm stopped in front of the scorpion.

"Come to Daddy," he said.

"Yeah, that's right," Megan said in a hollow voice. "Go to Daddy." She reached out and agitated the scorpion with the mug. It climbed onto Eric's hand.

The creature turned and Megan pulled away. But she wasn't fast enough. With one quick flick, Eric tossed the arthropod onto her blouse.

Megan squealed and flicked the hideous bug onto the floor. The scorpion scuttled toward me, way too fast for comfort. Like a balking donkey, I backed into the doorman. He made an audible, "Oof." I feared if I tried to stamp on the creature, it would get up into my pant leg. Yanking off one of my athletic shoes, I ran up to the ugly creature and smashed it.

"Shit! Shit! Shit!" Eric was spinning around in the twist of his pants, swatting and batting at his head. "I'm stung."

The other scorpion was no longer visible. I moved forward with my shoe raised.

Eric glanced at the doorman, the smartest one of all of us since he'd remained in the hallway. Maybe because the guy was Cuban, Eric asked him, "Am I going to die?"

"Some day," the doorman said.

CHAPTER FORTY-TWO

Eric glared at the smart-ass doorman. His scalp burned and he felt woozy. He told himself his faintness could be from the insulin as much as the scorpion.

"Persons do not die from one sting," the doorman said. "Go wash where it stinged you."

"Thanks a lot." Eric didn't move. The other scorpion was loose in the neighborhood of his feet, might even be tangled in his pants. The private investigator had killed one scorpion and was advancing into the room with her shoe in hand. The best bet was to let her take care of business. Afterward he would scrub the top of his head. Megan stood high on the bed like a fuzzy angel floating over him. Her head was haloed with light.

He hadn't heard the elevator go down, but he heard it now, chugging to a stop on the fifth floor. Heavy steps clomped down the hallway.

The doorman stood aside to let two uniformed policemen

enter. Eric thought they were wearing berets. "I feel dizzy," he said. Keeping his feet planted on the floor, he closed his eyes, groaned and flopped onto the bed. The mattress jiggled as Megan climbed off the other side. He was tempted to peek at her face. Instead he threw in a twitch for good measure. Let her think he might be dying and she might be disappearing into the pit of a Cuban jail. When he did open his eyes, the room spun.

With a warning tone, the doorman told the officers something in Spanish, which included a word that sounded like scorpion.

"There it is!" The private investigator whacked her shoe against the floor three times. The whooshing air fanned his calves.

One of the policemen barked an order that included the word *doctor.*

Eric closed his eyes again. Truth be told, he didn't feel so hot. Seeing a doctor sounded like a good idea. Much better than a trip to headquarters. Not that he'd committed a single crime.

CHAPTER FORTY-THREE

When the Cubana plane was airborne and I was still alive, I accepted the complimentary rum. Megan didn't respond to the stewardess. She kept her eyes averted, peering out the tiny window to the tarmac even though it was dark night. With the airport's minimal illumination, I knew there wasn't much for her to see. She had remained mute ever since we had been asked to leave the country and had been driven to the airport by a police escort, more, I think because of Megan's expired visa than because of the events in Hotel Ambos Mundos.

Personally, I was eager to leave Cuba while they believed that Eric's condition was the result of an accidental scorpion sting. Neither Megan nor I disabused them of the "accidental" part. Nor did the doorman. It was possible that, from the hallway, he hadn't seen all the action. Or maybe like so many witnesses, when he calmed down after his adrenaline-fueled heroics, he realized he didn't want to be involved. And, it was sort of an accident.

When the officer had escorted us to the ticket counter and afterward to the gate, Megan didn't comment on the birds flapping around in the terminal, pecking up crumbs of food on the floor and pooping on the plastic benches. I asked the policeman about the birds. He explained, a little embarrassed, I thought, that the birds had entered through a small hole in the ceiling, but couldn't find their way out. The problem had apparently existed for a while.

Megan swept along beside me, the hem of her skirt filthy. Neither of us smelled too dainty. It had been a long, long day.

Now on the small plane, I took a sip of my dark rum. It was god-awful sweet. Megan remained sullen for someone who'd escaped the fate of a Cuban jail. Dirt rimmed the neckline of her white blouse and her eyes were blurry. Of course, if I had cancer and was returning to a mother like Lucille, I might be on the glum side, too. But since I was me, I thanked our lucky stars.

The drink allowed me to relax enough to think back over the events of the previous night. One of the police officers had hoisted Eric onto his shoulder and demanded the help of the doorman. Megan sank onto the bed, her face pale and blank. Her body curled around her heart. Together, the two men dragged Eric off, presumably to a doctor, or a hospital. To me, that was neither here nor there. The son-of-a-bitch could die and I wouldn't feel a pang. Or should I say sting?

I didn't know if a half dose of insulin and a scorpion sting could do the job, but one could hope.

The other officer, who seemed in charge, remained in the room. He had an inch or two on my five foot eight but his light blue shirt and dark blue pants bagged on his slender frame. Belted around his middle were the accouterments of law enforcement everywhere. He repeatedly touched his pencil mustache as he peppered Megan and me with questions and scribbled notes: Names? Addresses in Cuba? Identification?

I produced my passport. Megan mumbled she didn't have hers. That seemed like utter stupidity. I translated in case the officer had not already inferred her response. He let her answer ride for the moment.

A package of cigarettes bulged in his shirt pocket and I wondered if smoking on the job was allowed down here. Could the officer have a rebellious streak? Or was he just another worker who received the same pay as everybody else and therefore did not care much about the finer points of his job? As if reading my mind, he extracted the package, tapped out a smoke, and flicking a match with his thumbnail, lit up.

"How did the scorpions get into the room?" The officer glanced at the crushed exoskeletons oozing innards and wrinkled his nose. He stepped over to the open air as smoke jetted from his nostrils. He threw the match out the opening.

I translated for Megan as though the question had nothing to do with me, like I had no idea how the creatures had made their way to the hotel. I had no doubt they had been taken from the clinic and Eric was the culprit.

She gazed at the floor and shrugged her fragile shoulders. "Eric had them. They got loose."

I repeated her response in Spanish. The officer didn't find the words worthy of comment. Holding his cigarette with his teeth, he snapped on one latex glove. He took a couple of puffs with his free hand. He came around the bed and pinched up the handle of the syringe. "What is in here?" He asked the question to the top of Megan's head.

I translated, happy to have a Beginning Spanish type question.

"Insulin," Megan murmured.

"*¿Insulina?*"

"Eric's diabetic." She twisted, and looked right at the policeman, her eyes doe-like, her face soft and vulnerable.

I was astounded by the ease and grace with which she lied. The word in Spanish was *diabético*, so the officer didn't need any help to understand. He placed the hypodermic back where he had found it. I wasn't sure why. Maybe because it would poke a hole in a baggy, or maybe a special team would arrive to collect the evidence. The officer looked around the room for other interesting evidence. He picked up the latex glove on the orange bedspread. "What is this for?" he asked in Spanish. Was he blushing? Perhaps to cover his embarrassment, he took a long drag on his cigarette.

I relayed Megan's answer—it had been stretched over the mug as a lid to contain the scorpions.

That was probably the truth, but it sounded less believable than her lie.

He went to the window, pinched the tip of his cigarette, and tossed it down to the street. "*Vámonos*," he said. "Let's go."

I started to perspire. He herded us to the elevator and down to the front desk where he engaged in a rather long and flirtatious conversation with the young receptionist, telling her that the room was to remain locked and undisturbed. From there, he'd steered us to a police car.

My stomach fluttered.

"Where is this Casa Tranquilidad?" he asked.

He understood the address without translation and seemed almost apologetic about asking us to sit in the back. However, he seemed less so when he discovered Megan's expired visa. He told her to collect her belongings. From there, we traveled to Casa Maria to pick up my things with the officer escorting me up the four flights, leaving Megan locked in the back of the patrol car. Now that I thought about it, there didn't seem to be a back way out of the building, not that I contemplated an escape. If the police wanted me to return to the United States, and to take Megan with me, I couldn't have been more delighted.

On the way up to Casa Maria, I explained to my escort that my visa was valid, but I had no objection to leaving.

"That's good," he said in Spanish.

Maria's face wrinkled at the sight of an officer standing in her living room. She wrung her hands even as I told her it was nothing to worry about—that I was leaving. I thanked her and went to my room to retrieve my suitcase. Since I had never unpacked, that took about one minute. I seized the opportunity to use the bathroom. On the way out, I asked Maria if Briget and Ingrid were there. She told me they'd gone to a club to listen to music.

"Please tell them goodbye from me," I said in Spanish.

I wished that I were them, visiting Cuba in a way that would allow me to take in the sights and sounds.

Instead, Megan and I spent the entire night in a dingy police station seated on hard plastic chairs. There was a lot of smoking and hand wringing and sighs and questioning. Megan stuck to her story. Eric was her diabetic boyfriend and she had no idea how the scorpions got in the room. The police must have confirmed the contents of the hypodermic. In the end we were driven along the freeway through the dark countryside to the airport where we waited with our police escort for the ticket window to open.

In the little jet, I lifted my plastic cup as if in a toast. *Adiós, Cuba.* I drank to a country of resourceful people who kept alive fifty-year-old cars and eked out profits by playing musical chairs with their rooms. Here's to the rhythm of music on the street, and to Castro's pristine coral reefs. The sweet liquid slid down my throat and warmed my belly. I lifted my cup again. Here's to the indomitable spirit of Cuba that chose life in spite of the stacked odds.

And here's to me, for another successful mission.

CHAPTER FORTY-FOUR

We did face the problem of reentering the United States. Megan seemed blasé about it—completely unconcerned. I was clammy nervous. Gus, the friend of a friend of J.J.'s, had said a person could stick a twenty in his/her passport and ask the Mexican customs officer not to stamp it. That way, there would be only one stamp into Mexico, instead of one right after the other with no indication a person had left. Two stamps into Mexico would be a problem if I stepped up to an alert U.S. customs officer who wanted to know where I'd been between times. I'd be faced with the dilemma of lying to a customs officer or admitting that I'd travelled to Cuba.

The line of Mexican customs officials stirred a bad feeling about trying a bribe. It felt like the United States' high alert after 9/11 had made its way to Mexico. Two head honchos patrolled back and forth in front of the booths, keeping their eyes on the female customs officers.

That was the other problem. My boyfriend David held the notion that because women had to scrabble to advance in the work place, they tended to be more rigid and by the book. I'd objected to his belief as pure sexism, but he had an annoying habit of being right. Now a row of booths stretched before me, every one of them filled with a woman. I extracted the twenty-dollar bill from my passport. I would request that the officer not stamp it and see what happened. "It never hurts to ask," my mom would say. Of course, that was after she had said, "No."

The next available officer had a down-turned mouth and gestured brusquely. "Please go ahead," I said to the couple behind us.

The next booth that cleared contained a younger woman and I stepped toward it. Megan hung back. I had to grab her wrist and pull her forward like a resistant child.

I smiled at the officer, greeted her in Spanish, and handed her my passport.

She said nothing. She thumbed through the booklet and raised her stamp.

"*Favor de no marcar mi pasaporte,*" I said.

"*¿Que?*"

That wasn't even the polite way of asking "What?"

She frowned at me.

I repeated my request, hoping the problem was with my Spanish.

"*Si usted no quiere una estampa, se puede regresar a Cuba.*"

She had just told me that if I did not want a stamp, I could go back to Cuba.

She waved over one of the pit bosses. I could feel the sweat beading on my forehead.

"*No, no, no,*" I pleaded. "*Estampe el pasaporte.*" I was desperate, but even as the boss approached, I tried, "*Detrás, detrás, por favor.*" My Spanish had gone all to hell, but I was trying to persuade her to stamp it in the back.

"*Voy a estamparlo donde quiero,*" she said. This meant I

will stamp it where I want, and with that she did. The stamp smacked loudly right on the front page. She folded her arms across her blue shirt, and as her boss arrived at the booth, she asked so he could hear. *"¿Quieres hablar con mi jefe?"* Do you wish to speak to my supervisor?

I gave the man my best smile. He was about my height, middle-aged, barrel-chested with stocky legs. He did not smile back.

"¿Hay un problema?"

He was asking if there was a problem, and for me, at the moment, there sure was, but I stammered, "*No. No hay ningún problema. Todo está bien.*" Nope. There was no problem. Everything was hunky dory.

Scowling, the female officer snapped up Megan's passport and stamped it with equal force. *"Bienvenidas a México."*

Welcome to Mexico.

In the Cancun airport, I led Megan into a bathroom. "Clean up, change your clothes, and get rid of anything that links you to Cuba." I'd already left my guidebook at Casa Maria.

"Who died and made you God?" She heaved a sigh.

However, she plopped her bag on the floor, unzipped it, and started stuffing items into the trash container.

She held up a pair of jeans and a long-sleeved tee with a glittery Santa Cruz on the front. "How's this, boss?"

"Perfect."

While she slipped into a stall, I flipped through the file her mother had given me, fished out sheets with references to Cuba, ripped them to shreds and stuffed them into the garbage can. When I had finished, I freshened up at the sink.

Megan emerged, the pink shirt reflecting color onto her face and the form fitting jeans accentuating legs that ran up to her chest. She threw the dirty white clothing into the garbage and washed up at the sink. Pulling a bright floral scarf from her bag, she proceeded to wrap it around her head and tie it, leaving the ends to drape fashionably around her shoulders. She stood before the mirror and applied mascara and a high gloss raspberry-colored lipstick. Before my eyes, she transformed into a thin, fragile-looking fashion model.

As we strolled back into the terminal, I noticed more spring in her step, but maybe it was only that she no longer had a skirt whipping around her legs. Since the Cuban government had only concerned itself with us getting out of Cuba, we now had to find two tickets back to San Jose, California. We got very lucky and found two middle seats, a couple of rows apart, on a flight leaving in three hours. I wanted to call David, but my trip to Cuba had been so short, he wouldn't even be back yet from visiting his son in Los Angeles. That didn't seem possible, but it was true. Unfortunately, I had not brought Abraham's number with me and David was allergic to cell phones. In spite of our problems, I felt how eager I was to share my tales with him and to hear about his trip.

In a moment of inspiration, I ducked into an airport souvenir shop and bought a baseball cap. I didn't wear baseball caps, especially not pink ones with a rainbow CANCUN on the front. But I had learned from Eric Mars that people see what they expect to see. At the clinic, he had stood right in front of me, shooting the breeze, hidden by a primitive disguise. The hat would be my disguise. Megan and I would be arriving in the United States with an airplane full of tourists from Cancun. I wanted to blend in.

Before our departure from Cancun, we had time to fuel up at a Starbucks. I scarfed down a huge scone with my coffee while Megan spooned up a yogurt. She wasn't talkative. Since I was not a chatty person either, we ate in silence, people watching, and slowly I realized we shared similar natures. We were both people who sat quietly and observed the world. Like me, Megan blatantly stared at people, sometimes to the point that they turned from their magazine, or raised a head from a cooing baby and frowned at the two of us.

After we ate, I bought a Sue Grafton murder mystery, and we made our way to the gate. The first leg of our trip was uneventful. I was wedged between two guys. A young one with disheveled dark hair slept against the window. With his mouth hanging open, he looked like he was passed out and I imagined him in Cancun for one continuous party. The middle-aged man on the aisle had a big beer belly that lifted up his Cancun tee shirt, rolling the top of the palm tree design into a crease and revealing a roll of fat above his shorts. Sniffing, I leaned one direction and then the other, trying to decide which of the two emitted the odor of dirty feet.

We'd be flying into Arizona, which made me think of my father. I'd tracked him down to the Arizona desert. It was a painful chapter in my life that I didn't want to think about.

"How'd you like Cancun?" the man on the aisle asked.

"It was fun." I poked my nose into the paperback. However, as much as I liked Grafton, she couldn't hold my attention. I checked my purse to make sure there was not an incriminating CUC stuck somewhere and opened my passport to inspect the stamps into Mexico.

I indicated to the man on the aisle that I needed to get out.

"Powder your nose?" he asked with a smile.

"Exactly."

I walked back to Megan's row and motioned for her to join me in the aisle. She was sandwiched between tan, blonde girls, who looked like they were teenagers. The minute Megan stood up they leaned together and chatted. I'd thought Megan was lucky, but maybe not. It couldn't be fun to be crammed between people who wanted to talk to each other, but were not willing to sit in a middle seat to do so.

"If the customs officer asks about the weather," I said in a low voice to Megan, "we simply say it was warmer than Santa Cruz."

She heaved a sigh. "Try to relax." She was a seasoned globetrotter, so none of this seemed to rattle her. I was the rookie traveler.

I returned to my seat and tried again to read my paperback. I couldn't focus and resumed worrying.

When our plane landed in Arizona, I plopped the pink Cancun cap on my head. I wanted Megan and me to look like everybody else on the plane, tourists returning from a winter trip to the resort city.

We approached a young customs officer who studied Megan's shirt. He was a tall, broad-shouldered guy in her age bracket. I couldn't blame him for checking her out.

I handed him my passport, thankful that my hand held steady. As he snapped open my passport, I held my breath.

He pointed at my address. "Santa Cruz," he said. He turned to Megan and beamed. "I wondered when I saw your shirt. I went to Santa Cruz High. Used to surf at The Point."

"Harbor High," Megan said.

"Really? Did you know Coach Smith?"

I leaned back and relaxed as the two took a brief walk down memory lane. Our customs officer led the way. I witnessed first hand what people had said about Megan. She answered his questions, but hung back shyly, as though unsure of what should come next. But it didn't matter. The guy had an open friendly nature, nice smile, and eagerness to talk about Santa Cruz. No doubt the surf was calling to him as he spoke. My heartbeat slowed into a regular beat. They'd make a cute couple.

He finally asked the *de rigueur* customs question, "Did you enjoy your stay in Cancun?"

"It was a blast," Megan said.

She lied so well. It was breathtaking.

The guy nodded at my hat. "Souvenir?"

"Yup," I said, keeping it short because I was not a good liar. I didn't need a reminder of this trip.

The guy glanced at my passport, stamped it and handed it back. He studied Megan's passport a little longer, but I had every sense that was so he could store her name in his memory bank.

Megan grabbed the handle of her suitcase and I tipped my hat at the guy. Eric Mars was right; people see what they expect to see.

On this stretch of our journey to San Jose Airport, Megan and I were able to sit together. Because of her cancer and her long legs, I offered her the aisle seat. An older Hispanic gentleman completed our row at the window. I felt a sweep of relief. With my worry gone, exhaustion moved in to occupy its space. I reclined my chair and let my mind roam. I thought about our expectations. The placebo effect worked because of expectation. Could it play a part with the blue scorpion venom cure? Expectation was powerful.

But expectation also made us vulnerable to scum like Eric Mars. He read people's expectations and used them to manipulate. Because I did not expect to see him, he had paraded right in front of my face.

In life, was it better to have expectations to pull us forward, to help us to achieve, or was it better to have no expectations, to let each moment hold its own value?

I fell into a slumber and missed the drink cart. When I lifted my head, Megan got up and made her way down the aisle. I seized the chance to stand up. She passed through first class and slid into their toilet. On her return, she stopped at the flight attendants' station. She sashayed back to our row with two cups of water, and I watched the way people noticed her as she glided by. *Could the venom have cured her cancer?* She seemed delicate, but strong, like a reed.

I sat back down and gulped the water. It tasted bitter, but it was wet. "Thank you. That hit the spot."

In San Jose, the flight attendant shook me awake. "Miss. We're in San Jose."

I lifted my eyelids. My seat had returned to its upright position and my head was dropped forward. It felt like a bowling ball. The window seat passenger in my row waited next to me, wanting to get out. The older gentleman had been too courteous to wake me or to climb over my body.

I blinked and looked around. Where was Megan? I sprang up, instantly feeling dizzy. Except for the older man, the crew, and me, the plane was empty. I held onto the top of a seat and remained standing so the patient old gentleman could get by.

Megan was gone. What had I expected? This made complete sense. She had no desire to see Lucille, and, I realized, unless Eric Mars died in Cuba, Megan was not safe from him, especially not back in Santa Cruz.

The last passenger on the plane, I took down my bag. On the way out, I asked the flight attendant when the plane had landed.

"Four fifty-two," she said brightly. "Right on time."

"Thanks." I would report to Lucille that as of 4:52 today, Megan was alive and roaming the earth.

I'd done my job.

CHAPTER FORTY-FIVE

J.J. summoned me to the office—an unusual event. I presumed he wanted the lo-down on the Cuban case. During the short drive, I steeled myself for criticism. J.J. wouldn't like that Megan had disappeared although he wouldn't care deeply as long as we were paid.

The weird non-alignment of the lanes on Soquel Drive didn't allow my mind to stray too far. When I reached our building, I was still marshaling my defenses. The hallway competed with the slums of Old Havana for dreariness. I pushed open the door into the familiar odor of burnt coffee.

Behind his desk lamp, J.J. glowed with showered freshness. He was spiffed up in a striped dress shirt accented with a dark blue tie.

"Court?" I asked.

He swept his hand toward my desk. "Have a seat."

The simple words stopped me cold. *Have a seat* was for bad

news.

J.J. waved his hand, less patiently. "Sit down," he said curtly. "Nobody died."

Dampness crept under my armpits before my rump hit the chair. I swiveled toward him.

In his pool of light, J.J. leaned back and propped his feet on his desk, his shoes shiny black under the lamp.

"New shoes?" I stabbed for casual, although his actions were not good signs.

Out of the circle of light, his face remained blank, a skill at which he had me beat. He was unreadable in court and a great detective when he could keep his act together. He scratched his chin, a small tell. Something was really bothering him. Maybe the check from Lucille had bounced.

After a few seconds that seemed like an eternity, he said, "You know I have a sponsor?"

"I didn't know," I said, "but I figured. That's part of the deal."

"He's a lawyer."

"Sounds like a good fit."

"Yeah." J.J.'s speculative gaze moved over my face and then dropped to my desk.

Holy shit. Something was wrong here. And for once, I didn't think it had to do with me. I ran my hand through my short hair, partly to dry my palm. "What's going on J.J.?"

J.J. lowered his legs and tilted forward in his chair, his serious demeanor now in the spotlight. He palmed a new orange stress ball and squeezed. "Gift from my sponsor."

Whatever news he had to impart, I realized, would have been easier for him with a drink. Instead he resorted to clenching and unclenching the pliable rubber.

"He offered me a job."

Not a case. Not a client. But I refused to believe.

He tossed me the ball. I reached and caught it with a steadiness that belied the knot in my stomach.

"So this is not about Cuba?"

J.J. shook his head. "Nah. Good job on that."

A compliment? There was no more denying that something was seriously wrong.

"What do you mean a job?"

"You know, to work for him." An edge of sarcasm snuck back into his voice.

I pitched the ball at his face. J.J. snatched it from the air. He grew up playing ice hockey and all his years of drinking had not dulled his reflexes. His mug twisted into a mask of pure disdain. "Their office is only big enough to support the services of one private detective."

"Are you selling the business?"

He guffawed. He stretched out his arm, the orange globe at his fingertips. He swiveled in his desk chair, pointing his arm like a horizontal Olympic torch in an arc about the gloomy room. My desk, a wire rack of forms, a metal file cabinet. Obsolete telephone, outdated answering machine and a slow computer. A copying machine. A counter with an old coffee pot and battered microwave. "The lease is up at the end of the year and I'm not renewing."

"So you're giving me the boot? I'm out of a job?"

"Unless you want to take over this shit heap, that's about it."

My body numbed with shock. The money from my private investigating wasn't much, but it filled the gaps left by working part-time as a baker. What would I tell David? I gulped at the idea. Even with the sale of our two former residences, we scrimped to pay our new mortgage.

I had no interest in returning to full-time baking at Archibald's, if that was even a possibility. Biting my lip, I blinked, feeling incipient tears, which was downright humiliating.

"Want this?" J.J. tossed me the stress ball.

I palmed the rubber and pressed it against the desk surface.

I stood and pushed all my weight into the rubber as though I could flatten it into a mold of my feelings, which felt smashed by a truck.

I tried to smile at J.J. but my lips twitched. "I guess we'll be competitors."

"Competitors?" J.J. snorted, crossed his arms over his chest and leaned back. "Don't let your limited success go to your head, honey. You're hardly competition for me."

J.J.'s gibe was an act of kindness. It stirred up my indignation and rebalanced my world. I would whoop his sorry ass in the grand future for Carolina Guadalupe Sabala, Private Investigator.

Because Cuban people lack so many resources, Cuban black beans can sometimes be a little bland. My friend Huve Rivas supplied the following recipe. He hails from Puerto Rico and this is an adaptation of his mom's recipe. The people of Puerto Rico like their black beans a little more soupy than the people of Cuba. These are truly delicious!

Black Bean Recipe

2 tsp. olive oil

1 pound of black beans

1 8 oz. can tomato sauce

sofrito (sautéed onion, cilantro, clove of garlic, 1 bell pepper, lots of cilantro in olive oil)

10-12 olives (pimiento stuffed)

1 tbs. capers

2 cubed medium-sized potatoes

Enough water to keep an inch or two above beans while cooking

salt to taste

Some people add a tsp. of ground cumin

- Rinse beans and let them soak in a pot of water for overnight to soften. (Use whatever water is not absorbed for cooking.)
- Lightly sauté sofrito
- In a large pot place beans and cover with water and bring to a boil. Lower flame to bring them to simmer.
- Add salt and sofrito (you can add extra raw cilantro), and let it simmer for about 20-30 min.
- Then add potatoes, olives, capers, and tomato sauce.
- Cook for another 30 to 40 minutes or until beans are tender.
- Don't let the water level go below beans.
- Gently stir every once in a while.
- Some people simmer beans without a cover while others cover with a lid.

Serves 8

ACKNOWLEDGMENTS

I owe many thanks to the organizers of Killer Nashville who selected *Black Beans & Venom* as a Claymore Award finalist, opening opportunities for whole novel feedback from several publishers. Also valuable was the on-line critique group set up through Sisters in Crime Guppies. I had the privilege of working with mystery author Andrew MacRae, and up-and-comers Connie Berry, Susan Bickford, and Karen Hutchinson.

My niece, Patricia Denke, a doctor of entomology, contributed some scorpion facts for this book. Patricia Rain allowed me use of her journal to help with the babalao scenes. As a person interested in folk remedies, Patricia Rain may have been the first person to tell me about blue scorpion venom.

Joyce Crain and Sue Lundquist provided invaluable early proofreading, and Huve Rivas supplied the recipe for the most delicious black beans I've ever tasted! I am indebted to the fine ladies at misterio press for taking me on as an author. And finally, this mystery could not have been written without my fearless fellow traveler, Daniel Friedman.

ABOUT THE AUTHOR

In addition to the Carol Sabala mystery series, Vinnie Hansen pens short stories. Her mystery short story *Novel Solution* will appear in *Fish or Cut Bait*, the third Guppy anthology to be published by Wildside Press in 2015.

Vinnie lives in Santa Cruz, California, with her husband, abstract artist Daniel S. Friedman. Please visit her website at http://vinniehansen.com. She's also on Facebook and Goodreads.

VINNIEHANSEN.COM

Made in the USA
San Bernardino, CA
06 May 2016